CATACOMB

MADELEINE ROUX

HARPER

An Imprint of HarperCollins*Publishers*

For Andrew & Kate

Catacomb

Copyright © 2015 by HarperCollins Publishers

All rights reserved. Printed in the United States of America.

www.epicreads.com

Library of Congress Cataloging-in-Publication Data
Roux, Madeleine, date.
    Catacomb / Madeleine Roux. — First edition.
        pages   cm.
    Sequel to: Sanctum.
    Summary: Dan, Abby, and Jordan embark on a senior road trip to New
Orleans, but as creepy occurrences escalate into near-death experiences,
the trio realizes they will be lucky to make it out of this senior trip alive.
    ISBN 978-0-06-236405-0 (hardback)
    ISBN 978-0-06-242689-5 (special edition)
    ISBN 978-0-06-241445-8 (int.)
    ISBN 978-0-06-244492-9 (special edition)
    [1. Supernatural—Fiction. 2. Automobile travel—Fiction. 3. Haunted
places—Fiction. 4. Horror stories.] I. Title.
PZ7.R772Cat 2015   2015005624
[Fic]—dc23   CIP
                                                AC

Typography by Faceout Studio

15 16 17 18 19 CG/RRDC 10 9 8 7 6 5 4 3 2 1

❖

First Edition

"In the province of the mind,
what one believes to be true either is true
or becomes true."

—John Lilly

"Men are not prisoners of fate,
but only prisoners of their own minds."

—Franklin D. Roosevelt

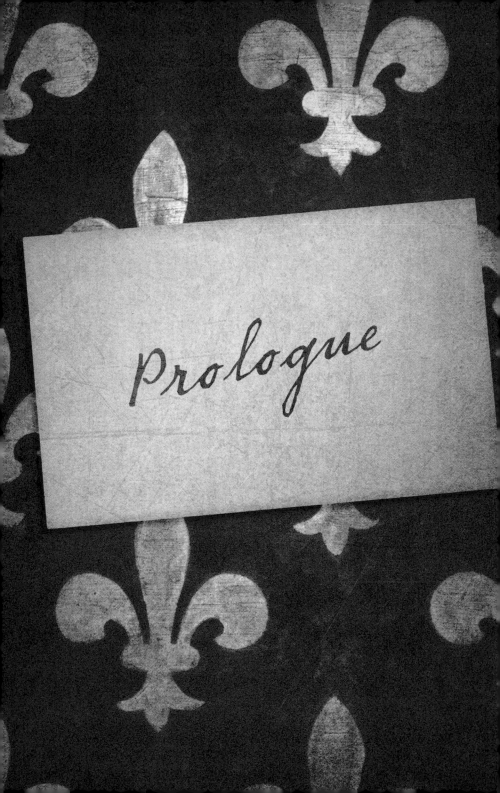

Prologue

These were the rules as they were first put down:

First, that the Artist should choose an Object dear to the deceased.

Second, that the Artist feel neither guilt nor remorse in the taking.

Third, and most important, that the Object would not hold power until blooded. And that the more innocent the blood for the blooding, the more powerful the result.

Chapter 1

*A*t first the idea of a cross-country road trip had been hard to stomach. If sleeping in a tent wasn't horrible enough, Dan had felt anxious, almost sick, at the prospect of being away from his computer, his books, his *alone time* for two whole weeks. But that was the deal Jordan offered when he wrote to them with the big news: he was moving to New Orleans to live with his uncle.

Perfect chance, his email had said, *to have some time together. You two nerds can help me move down there, and we'll get a last hurrah before we all traipse off to college.*

Dan couldn't argue with that, or with any reason to spend more time with Abby. She'd visited him in Pittsburgh once a few months ago, and they'd been talking online more or less every week. But two weeks away from parents and chaperones . . . He didn't want to get ahead of himself, but maybe their relationship could finally flourish, or at least survive, with some much-needed quality time together.

The Great Senior Exodus, Jordan had called it. And now, a day after leaving Jordan's miserable parents behind in Virginia, the trip was finally starting to live up to that name.

"These are incredible," Jordan was saying, flicking through the pictures Abby had taken and then uploaded onto his laptop

for safekeeping. "Dan, you should really check these out."

"I know it's kind of cliché, photographing Americana in black and white, but lately I've been obsessing over Diane Arbus and Ansel Adams. They were the focus of my senior project, and Mr. Blaise really loved it."

Dan leaned forward between the seats to look at the photographs with Jordan. "They're definitely worth the stops," he said. They really were something. Open landscapes and deserted buildings—through Abby's eyes, they were desolate, but also beautiful. "So Blaise finally gave you an A, then?"

"Yup. No more stupid A minuses for me." She beamed. Jordan offered up a high five, which Abby managed without taking her eyes off the road. "He actually grew up in Alabama. He's the one who gave me ideas for sites to photograph."

They had already stopped a few—well, *many*—times to allow Abby to take photos, but Dan didn't mind the extra time on the road. He could ride forever in this car with his friends, even if his turns driving got a little tedious.

"I know it's lame to take us so far out of the way, but you're not in too much of a hurry to get there, are you, Jordan?"

"You've already apologized about a million times. Don't worry about it. I'd say something if it was annoying."

"Yes," she said with a laugh. "I'm sure you would."

If he was honest, Dan wasn't in too much of a hurry to get there, either.

It had been nine months since they'd watched the Brookline asylum burn to the ground. The three of them had barely escaped with their lives, and they'd managed that much only with the help of a boy named Micah, who had died trying to buy them time to escape their pursuers. Micah had had a rough, short life, and he'd grown up in Louisiana—a fact Dan had never told Abby or Jordan. Now, just when it seemed like the ghosts of the past were finally content to leave Dan and his friends alone, the three of them were headed to the most haunted city in America. It felt like they were tempting fate, to say the least.

"You okay back there?" Abby asked, cruising smoothly down Highway 59.

"Yeah, I'm good, Abs," Dan said. He wasn't sure if that was a lie. But before Abby could call him on it, Jordan's phone dinged—or rather, a clip of Beyoncé fired off loud enough to make all three of them jump.

Dan knew what that meant. "You're still talking to Cal?"

"On and off," Jordan said, quickly reading the text message. "The on part is why Mom won't pay for school. Not sure what I'd do without Uncle Steve."

"You could stop talking to Cal," Dan suggested.

"And let my parents *win*? Not likely." He peered around the center console at Dan, his bare feet propped up on the dashboard. Late afternoon sunlight glinted off the shiny new black lip piercing Jordan had insisted on getting in Louisville. "He says physical therapy is a real shit show sometimes, but his life feels like paradise after New Hampshire College. Hey! I just realized that at Uncle Steve's, I'll be able to Skype with him without my mother the drama queen bursting into tears."

Dan shifted again, even antsier now at the mention of New Hampshire College. If he let his mind wander or dwell, he would feel the heat of the flames that had engulfed Brookline and everything in it. He wanted to believe that Brookline's effect on him had ended that day—that the evil had died with Warden Crawford and Professor Reyes—but his last moments at the college had given him cause to doubt.

He'd had another vision. He'd seen Micah's ghost, waving good-bye.

He hadn't had any visions since then, and for that, Dan was grateful. It felt like a signal: it was time to let it all go and move on. Even the files and journals he had saved from the ordeal held no interest anymore.

Well, except for one small thing.

Before the trip, Abby and Jordan had threatened to subject Dan to a search of his things for any junk he might have brought from Brookline. They'd said it like a joke—like, no way Dan would really do that to them, right?

But in the end, they hadn't dumped out his bag, which meant they hadn't found the file he had brought along. The one that had been folded in half at the bottom of the stack they'd rescued from Professor Reyes's things. The one labeled *POSSIBLE FAMILY / CONNECTIONS?*, inside which he'd found a paper-clipped pile of papers, connected by a name that had made his heart shoot into his mouth.

MARCUS DANIEL CRAWFORD.

Nine months ago, that pile of papers had seemed like a gift, the reward at the end of a long, hard search for answers about his mysterious past. A sparse family tree had confirmed what he'd already suspected: Marcus was his father, and he was also the nephew of the warden through the warden's youngest brother, Bill. But a single line had also been drawn from Marcus to someone named Evelyn. Was that his mother? It seemed so incomplete. He'd tried to find any Evelyn Crawford online who seemed like a match, but with no promising results and no maiden name, he hadn't had much else to go on.

There was more in the stack—an old postcard, a map, even a police report detailing a time his father had been arrested for breaking and entering—but maddeningly, nothing that would help him pick out his father from the numerous Marcus Daniel Crawfords he found online, and nothing else about his potential mother.

Still. Even after the pile of papers had come to feel less like a gift than a curse, he'd kept the folder hidden. And when he'd packed his bags for this trip, the thought of Paul and Sandy going through his room and finding the folder had been enough to make him bring it—to keep it in sight.

As if on cue, Dan's phone buzzed, not with Beyoncé but with the more subdued jingle indicating Sandy was texting. He checked the message, smiling down into the faint glow of the screen.

How are the intrepid roadtrippers doing? Please tell me you are eating more than beef jerky and Skittles! Call at the next good stopping place.

Dan texted back to reassure her that they were doing their best to eat actual, normal food.

"How's Sandy?" Jordan asked, craning around to look at him again.

"She's good. Just making sure we aren't stuffing ourselves with junk the whole way to Louisiana," Dan replied. He flicked his eyes up to see Jordan swallowing with some difficulty—the insides of his lips were a guilty shade of Skittles orange.

"It's a road trip. What does she think we're going to do?" Jordan asked. "Boil quinoa on the radiator?"

"That's not a half-bad idea," Abby teased. "We are *not* stopping at McDonald's tonight."

"But—"

"No. I checked to see if there was anything to eat other than fast food on the route. Turns out we can avoid the Montgomery traffic and stop at a cute little family-owned diner off 271."

"Diners have hamburgers," Jordan pointed out sagely. "So really, that doesn't change much."

"Hey, I'm just providing a few more options. What you stuff down your gullet is none of my business," she said.

"And thank God for that," Jordan muttered. "Quinoa is for goats."

"I'm with Abby," Dan said. "I could use a salad, or just, you know, a vegetable of any kind. I'm starting to shrivel up from all the beef jerky."

He heard the satisfied smile in Abby's voice as she sat up straighter in the driver's seat and said, "That's settled then. The place I found is called the Mutton Chop, and the same family has owned it for generations. We can get a little local history for my photography project *and* a decent meal."

"I'm still getting a burger," Jordan muttered. He twisted to face the windshield, sighing as he slid down into his seat and began to text at lightning speed. "Soon I'll be on the all-gumbo, all-jambalaya diet. Gotta get my burgers in while I still can."

Chapter 2

*W*hen the tire popping jolted Dan out of a nap, his first thought was to be grateful he wasn't the one driving.

"What was that!" Jordan had shot up like rocket, too, gripping the edge of the door while the car began to swerve and then slow.

"I think we lost a tire," Abby said with a sigh. She didn't seem frightened in the least, holding the wheel steady while the car corrected and then leveled out. She navigated them carefully off the road, letting the Neon idle in the ditch for a second before turning off the ignition. "And that's why you always pack a spare."

"What the hell are we going to do?" Jordan asked, leaning against the window to try to see which tire had blown.

"Paul taught me how to fix tires when I first learned to drive, but I doubt I could manage it," Dan said. They had cell signal, at least, so Triple-A was a possibility.

"Well, lucky for you boys, *I* practiced right before the trip." Patting the wheel with a smug little hop, Abby opened the door and circled to the trunk.

"There'll be no living with her after this," Jordan warned.

"Just be glad she can do it," Dan said. "It's getting dark."

"That's, um, not what I meant."

"Jordan? Jordan! Where is the spare? I know I checked it before I left New York. . . ." Her shout was muted through the windows, but still sharp and getting sharper.

"*That's* what I meant." Jordan sucked in a huge breath, steeling himself, and then eased out of the car. "So, um, before I explain anything, just promise you won't murder me."

"No deal," Abby said. Dan joined them in the cooling night air, watching them square off with matching crossed-arm poses. "Where's the spare, Jordan?"

"Funny story. Remember how my dad was rushing us out the door and I was like, oh, I totally do not need to bring my tauntaun sleeping bag? And then, in the end, I realized that yes, I absolutely, one hundred percent did need to bring it? I'm moving, Abby. Like, for good. I couldn't just leave my tauntaun sleeping bag behind."

Dan snorted behind his wrist, watching Abby's face pale with fury.

"You took out the spare tire to make room for your stupid *Star Trek* memorabilia?"

"Hey, whoa, whoa. I would *not* do that. Star *Wars* memorabilia, on the other hand . . ."

"Whatever it is!" Abby pinched the bridge of her nose, going to inspect the popped tire. She crouched, muttering to herself. "Great. We'll have to walk into town for a spare, then."

"Is it far?" Dan asked, getting out his phone to check the GPS. "Couldn't we just call a tow company?"

"That's way too expensive," Abby replied. "I'm already going to have to buy a new tire, and it's just a half mile more down the road. We almost made it. It wouldn't have been a big deal at all if smarty-pants over here hadn't packed like a twelve-year-old."

"There's nothing to fight about now," Dan said, putting a hand lightly on Abby's shoulder. "And I can kind of see his side. He *is* moving. If he wants New Orleans to feel like home, then he has to bring the stuff he cares about."

"Thank you, Dan. At least two of us understand the value of a tauntaun sleeping bag."

"*Stop saying it.*"

"What?" Jordan smirked. "Tauntaun sleeping bag?"

"Shut. Up. Every time you say that it just makes me want to punch you more," she said, shaking her head. But she was smiling. "That thing better be really warm at least. Maybe I'll borrow it tonight as payback."

Nobody had bothered to replace the burned-out neon lights that had once advertised the Mutton Chop. What few bulbs were left told Dan they were eating at the O CH P. The tiny gravel parking lot was packed with cars—mostly rusting trucks. Smoke poured out from some smokestack in the back, filling the air with the salty tang of a greasy-spoon grill.

A mechanic's shop was attached to the building. Not exactly appetizing for the diner, Dan thought, but pretty darn fortunate for them. Food could wait. Abby led them to the door of the garage, but it was dark inside. A scrap of paper on the window read Mechanic Next Door.

The sounds of clinking glasses, country jukebox music, and laughter reached them from the open diner window. A crooked placard next to the screen door seemed to Dan like a warning: "The Mutton Chop! Where everyone knows your face!"

"Where everyone knows your face? Isn't it *name*?" Jordan asked with a snort. "They couldn't even plagiarize properly."

"Don't be a snob, Jordan." Abby opened the screen door, holding it for the boys while they filed through.

"What are you, Saint Abby, protector of the hillbillies?" The noise coming from inside the diner managed to die out in the exact second Jordan finished his sentence. Two dozen heads turned in unison to stare at them. Dan didn't spy many smiles among the crowd. "Of which there are none in this oh-so-charming establishment," Jordan finished, clearing his throat.

"Please stop talking," Abby whispered, turning to address the man who'd walked over and now stood waiting to greet them. Mercifully, the rest of the diners went back to their business.

"Hi there, sir. We were wondering if you could get us the mechanic? Is he here? We blew a tire and need to buy a spare."

The man looked nice enough. He appeared to be in his early twenties, pudgy, and had a short, unkempt beard. He had a name tag that read *JAKE LEE* and grease stains on his coveralls.

"You're in luck, little lady. I'm the mechanic, and a damn good one at that, even if I am just a hillbilly," he said pointedly, shifting his gaze to Jordan. "So, you need a spare tire, eh? What kinda car y'all driving?"

Abby fell into conversation with him, following as he led them back toward the darkened mechanic's shop. She told him she drove a 2007 Neon, and she assured him she had the tools to do the job, just not the tire itself.

He went around to the back of the garage, and in no time at

all he returned with a tire, placing it on the ground in front of them with a heavy *whump*.

"It's getting late, and I'd feel bad letting y'all go back out there alone. You sure you know what you're doing?" He took off his baseball cap and ruffled his sparse hair. He looked directly at Abby, watching her struggle to roll the new tire onto its side.

"Could you give us a ride back to the car? I'd really appreciate it. We were planning to stop in the diner for dinner, but it'd be better if we could bring our car back here before it gets too dark."

Jake Lee nodded, then turned and marched off in the direction of his enormous pick-up. "Might be a tight squeeze. Truck's meant for haulin' stuff, not people."

"That's fine," Abby said. "Thanks for helping us out." Dan had no idea how she could keep up such a bright demeanor while she tried to maneuver the tire into the flatbed of the truck. Dan dashed over to help, and then Jordan joined, too.

"No trouble at all," Jake said.

Dan hoped this was just friendly Southern hospitality at work. He couldn't help feeling a creepy vibe from this guy and his willingness to help them. But it was already getting dark, and if they had to walk back to the car with that heavy tire it would take them way too long.

They piled into the front cab of the truck, Jordan whimpering from the sudden onslaught of about sixteen car fresheners stuffed behind the rearview mirror. "Maybe I'd rather walk," he whispered. "What smell do you think he's trying to cover up?"

"I'd rather not think about it," Dan whispered back.

Jake Lee drove them back up the road, humming softly as they

went. When that started to get weird, he turned on the radio, and bluegrass blasted out of the tinny speakers, so loud and frantic it immediately gave Dan a headache.

Abby remained all smiles, hopping out of the truck when they reached the Neon. Without prompting, Jake Lee parked and lowered the gate on the truck bed, grunting and sweating as he pulled the spare onto the gravel ditch.

"Here now," he said, lumbering back to the cab and getting an enormous flashlight. "Take this. You can give it back to me when you get in to the diner for supper."

"That's really nice of you," Abby said, fetching the little tool kit and jack from the back of the car. Dan heard her sigh at the sight of the sleeping bag rolled up where the spare tire ought to be. He took up the position of spotlight operator, holding the big yellow bulb steady while Abby set to work.

He glanced at Jake Lee, who had paused on the way back to his truck to watch them. More than watch them, really—he was staring, his head cocked to the side like he'd just discovered a rare species of insect and was trying to decide what to do with it. Dan tried to give a friendly wave to get his attention, but the mechanic just frowned and shook his head before driving off into the night.

Chapter

3

The tire change was taking longer than Dan expected. His arms were beginning to cramp from holding the flashlight steady.

"If I were a straight guy," Jordan said, "this would be a total turn-on." He took off his thick, fashionable glasses and wiped at his nose and forehead with his arm.

"Then not for the first time, I'm glad you're not straight," Dan said. "Jordan, you could at least try to help."

"I'd just get in the way," he said.

Abby gave a tiny grunt of effort, wrenching off another of the blown tire's lug nuts.

"Good thing that car only weighs about sixteen pounds max," Jordan added. This was met with a swift, blind kick from Abby, who was now pressed up against the car's faded, electric-green chassis.

"At least one of us knows how to change a freaking tire!" she shot back. Her forearms and face were streaked with war-paint lines of grease and dirt.

"Thanks, Mr. Valdez!" Dan said, crouching to see what she was working on. She had at last managed to maneuver the replacement into alignment. The only thing left to do was tighten the nuts on the spare.

"Thanks, *Mrs.* Valdez," Abby countered. "She's the one who insisted I learn this before even considering a road trip."

"Here," Dan offered, holding out his hand for the wrench. "Let me finish this."

"Are you sure?" she asked. She puffed back a wisp of purple hair. She had dyed a few streaks at the beginning of summer, and now her naturally black hair was encroaching down toward the roots.

"I think I can handle it," Dan said. "Righty tighty, lefty loosey? Anyway, the blood is running out of my arms. You take the flashlight."

They changed places, Dan kneeling next to the car while Abby positioned the flashlight to shine down onto his head and the tire. Tightening the tire onto the car was harder work than he expected, and he had to grip the wrench with both hands to gather enough force. Finally, he had to lower the car jack so he could finish.

"Wow, Jordan is right," Abby said. "That is kind of a turn-on."

Dan blushed, ruffling his hair shyly. "I think we're good to go. Let's get this stuff in the trunk and get back to the diner, yeah? I'm starving."

"If you insist," Jordan said with a sigh, helping Dan pack up the flashlight and tool kit. "At this point I'd prefer McDonald's. That mechanic was just a little too eager to help."

"I think he was nice," Abby said, climbing back into the driver's seat.

"Ugh. Careful," Jordan replied with a shudder. "I wouldn't let him hear you say that."

✗✗✗✗✗

When they returned to the diner, the atmosphere once again became quiet, almost chilly. Jake Lee was nowhere to be found, but the lights were still out in the garage next door, so Dan held on to the flashlight.

The service at the Mutton Chop was slow, although apparently not for the other tables. Dan watched platters of food come and go, but the only thing that had made it to their table was a cup of coffee for Abby, delivered by a man whose nametag read *Fats Buckhill*. Dan hadn't even gotten his water yet. Abby tapped her ringed fingers on the surface of the table and offered a friendly smile whenever Mr. Fats, the owner-slash-waiter-slash-horror-movie-extra, hobbled by the table, but he just kept saying, "I'll be right with you."

To be fair, for almost 9:00 p.m., the diner was surprisingly busy. Dan could swear every local in the joint was staring at them, but whenever he turned to see, they whipped back around, suddenly very interested in their food.

"This is how it starts," Jordan hissed, leaning in to get closer to Dan. Abby ignored him. "First that mechanic. There's always the one gruff yokel who warns you or has that *hee-haw* donkey laugh, and then everyone in the movie theater is all, *Get out! Get the hell out of there! What are you even thinking?*"

Dan snorted. Abby's sharp elbow founds its way into his ribs, but even she had a smile for Jordan's joke.

"Laugh it up," Jordan continued, all but hiding behind the big, laminated menu. "Who do you think they'll kill and feed to the pigs first? Duh, me. Of course they'll bump off the gay kid first. That's like redneck murder one-oh-one."

"That's just judgmental," Abby replied, sipping her jet-fuel coffee. It was one of her only vices—Dan had lost count of how many cups of coffee she'd had so far this trip. But if it kept her awake for the drive, more power to her. They still had a few hours to go tonight before they made it to the next campsite. "You don't know these people, Jordan, and even if they are a little less . . . cosmopolitan, there's nothing wrong with that. Your way of life isn't better or worse."

"False," Jordan declared, lowering his voice when he spotted the owner returning to check on them. "My way of life is objectively better because mine has Wi-Fi and Netflix."

"How y'all doin' here, then?" Fats Buckhill crouched to bring himself down to the table's level. His old knees cracked ominously as he did so, loud and crisp as breaking twigs. He had wide-set, friendly eyes under a heavy brow and a salt-and-pepper beard that was neat and closely shaven. One eye was slightly milky, the other crystal blue.

"Really good, Mr. Buckhill," Abby said politely. "I'm going to be getting the Cobb, and these two . . ." She trailed off, eyeing them impatiently.

"Burger," Jordan said shortly. His hand hovered in front of his mouth, probably trying to cover up his new piercing so the locals wouldn't judge him. "Bacon burger. Tons of bacon, just really go for it. And a milk shake if you've got 'em. Chocolate."

Fats laughed at that, cocking his head back. "Oh, I like you, son. You got good old-fashioned tastes."

Dan felt Abby's elbow jab preemptively, but that didn't stop his incredulous smile. "Oh, yes," Dan said with as much sincerity as he could muster, "Jordan is about as traditional as they come."

That earned him a kick under the table from both of them.

"The pulled pork and potato salad for me," Dan said, vowing to humor Abby and be less of a smart ass. "A Coke, too. And maybe a slice of the chess pie for later."

"Another sound decision-maker." Fats stood, his knees crackling again, and swept up their menus, tapping all three together like a deck of cards on the table.

"If it's not too much trouble," Abby added, clearing her throat resolutely, "would you mind sitting down to talk for a little while? I'm working on a photo project and it won't be complete without some insight from the people who actually live in and love these places."

She was laying it on thick, but it worked. Fats's one good eye twinkled. "Why of course, that'd be just fine. Let me put these orders in with Fats Junior and then I'll be right back to oblige you."

The old man shuffled away, perhaps with a bit more spring in his step now. The hush of the restaurant grew less pronounced, as if some secret signal that the teenagers were all right had been given.

"Did you see how cheery he got?" Jordan murmured. He kept his eyes glued to Fats. "Old fart's just excited I'm eating all that bacon. Gonna get me nice and plump before the slaughter."

Abby rolled her eyes and took a long swig from her coffee. "Well, after the year we've had, I understand why you're nervous, but we've earned some peace and quiet, Jordan," she said. "Some normalcy."

"Don't say shit like that. Don't! That's like catnip for bad juju."

Dan had already decided to stay out of it when he felt his phone vibrate in his pocket. Probably Sandy getting worried that he hadn't called her yet today. He checked his messages, finding the alert hadn't come from a text but from his Facebook app. Dan couldn't imagine who would be messaging him on Facebook. There wasn't anyone from his high school he planned to keep in touch with. Could it be one of his fellow freshman class members at Chicago saying hello?

He flicked the app open with his thumb, half-listening to his friends squabble. Fats returned, leaning onto the edge of the booth frame to chitchat with Abby.

Dan tabbed over to his inbox, feeling his hand freeze into a numb vice around the phone.

This wasn't right. Or okay. Or possible.

"Jimmy Orsini operated up and down this route during Prohibition, didn't he?" Abby was saying, and she even pulled out a photograph to show the restaurant owner. But she might as well have been speaking in tongues. "My teacher Mr. Blaise grew up around here, and he was telling me all about how interesting Orsini's grave is. I was going to try and get there, to photograph it. That's sort of my thing right now. Photography, I mean, not graves."

Fats's reply sounded distant, too, and Dan realized it was because his blood was pumping so loudly in his ears it was making it hard to hear. "I wouldn't recommend photographing that, little miss. Never know what that kind of thing might stir up. Bad energies and the like. There's a downright shivery ghost story about Orsini and his gang. The gravestone's in Alabama, sure enough, but the Pinkertons gave 'em hell all up and down this route—finally caught 'em down in New Orleans. Orsini got himself shot up in an escape attempt."

Yes. Ghost stories. *Ghosts.* That word at last pierced his brain. Dan stared down at the message and its sender, and he soundlessly mouthed the words back to himself.

Micah Bonheur
da Niel dani el
areu there ill
be se eing you real so on.

Chapter

4

*T*he food arrived while he was still staring down at his phone, but his appetite had fled. *Prank*, he thought. *I'll kill whoever did this*. His palms grew sweaty around the phone until he shoved it into his pocket. Out of sight, out of mind.

"You okay?"

Jordan stared at him, squinting while he sucked down his milk shake. Shrugging, Dan pushed a fork halfheartedly through his potato salad. He couldn't explain the message from Micah, especially not there, with Abby still chatting away with Fats. Now she was taking notes, scribbling names and places in between bites while the old man pulled up a chair next to the booth, apparently cozy enough for a long visit.

"Not sure the food's agreeing with me," Dan finally whispered. Just the smell of it made him sick now, anxiety turning his guts to acid.

Who would be cruel enough to play a prank like this? Certainly not Abby or Jordan, and as far as he knew, his twisted old roommate, Felix, was still locked away. He doubted the institution would let him have access to the internet, let alone social media. The only living person left who knew both Dan and Micah was Cal, a friend of Micah's from NHC who'd been a total dick to Dan and his friends last fall—to put it mildly. But according to Jordan, Cal had done a complete 180 in the months since then. Dan's mind spun, coming up empty.

"Can't blame you," Jordan said. "That potato salad looks kinda rancid. Want some of my fries?"

"Oh, uh, sure, yeah." He couldn't go through this again, lying to his friends. They always seemed to find out anyway. He'd tell them later, when they were alone. Dan forced a smile and took one of Jordan's fries. Then he rifled through his bag, grabbed his meds, and choked down one of the little blue pills with his soda. His disorder always got worse when he was feeling especially anxious.

"Long car rides make me sorta queasy, too," Jordan added. Then, all at once, he seemed to realize that the look on Dan's face had nothing to do with the food or the car ride. "Dan, what's wrong? It's something else, isn't it?"

Wasn't it always?

Dan scraped for an answer, his heartbeat speeding up. "I brought one of the files." Glancing at Abby, he lowered his voice. "You know, the *files*? I know we sorted through most of it at NHC, but I had to make sure I had seen it all. Because of my family history, you know?"

Jordan went a little green, lowering his milk shake. His big, dark eyes grew bigger behind his curly fringe. "Oh."

"Yeah. There's stuff in there about my dad, maybe my mom, too, but I can't be sure. I already went through it all, and I didn't really find anything concrete, just more dead ends."

"Why were their files mixed up in the professor's things?" Jordan whispered.

Dan gulped. He really hadn't meant to do this right here, right now, but now that he'd started talking, it was like this confession had been building behind a dam in his brain, waiting for the opportunity to be released.

"Remember how Professor Reyes said there were things I could see that other people couldn't?"

"I don't know—maybe? There was a lot going on that night."

"Well, I . . . You know what, never mind."

"Hey, I mean, if you need to talk about it," Jordan started, but suddenly Dan wasn't ready for that. This was not the right time, with Abby having a congenial conversation on one side and with hours still to go before another night in a tent.

"We should get going," he blurted, looking outside to find the kind of countryside darkness that was so dense it felt oppressive, even through glass. "It's late, and we wanted to get an early start tomorrow, right?"

Dan said it loudly enough for Abby to hear. She cleared her throat, glaring.

Luckily, Jordan was tired enough to yawn or loyal enough to fake it. "I'm beat, too, and we still have tents to set up."

Outnumbered, Abby gave in, but not before thanking Fats for all his time and information. She frowned at the boys as if they were in on some conspiracy against her. Which, technically, they were.

Dan gave her an apologetic smile. "Oh, Mr. Buckhill," he said, catching the man before he made it back to the kitchen. "Could you please give this flashlight to Jake Lee? We tried to catch him next door but the sign said he'd be over here."

Fats smiled. "Well, I would if I knew who Jake Lee was."

"Jake Lee . . . the mechanic?" Dan said, but his stomach was already twisting with dread. The realization dawned on him with sickening clarity: Jake had never asked them to pay for the tire.

"That man over there, Greg Mackey—if you need a mechanic, he's your guy."

Dan, Abby, and Jordan all looked at one another in silence. Gathering their bags quickly, they left the flashlight and a generous tip on the table before running out to the car and the night.

Chapter 5

"So what's our next stop tomorrow? You got any more side trips planned, Abs?" Jordan asked. They were trying to keep the mood light, but they were all thoroughly spooked. The headlights on the Neon picked up little beyond the oncoming road, the occasional sign, and the flashes of trees running just beyond the curb. "Not sure how much more of Tennessee I can take."

"Alabama," Abby corrected.

"Tennebamatucky, whatever. They all look the same at this point."

"We're still just outside Montgomery, Jordan, use your GPS," Abby snapped. Then she took a deep breath. "I guess the scenery *was* kind of similar all day, but that's what I'm going for with my project," she explained. "I bet when I line my photos up next to shots from thirty, forty, even a hundred years ago, there won't be much of a difference. I think it's fascinating. Time goes on but nothing really changes in some places. Kind of a nice thought, right? That some things are actually permanent. Reliable . . ."

She trailed off, her voice growing a little sad.

"Sure," Jordan said. "I get that. Doesn't mean it doesn't put me to sleep, but I hear you."

"You had better be awake now," Dan said. "You're helping set up the tent when we make it to the campground."

"I can't wait to get to Mobile tomorrow." Abby pressed on, slowing the car as signs for the Woods Campground flashed by in the headlights. "The Magnolia Cemetery is supposed to be a gold mine—so many incredible mausoleums there. Mr. Blaise said I can't miss it. I promise we won't stop long. I know we're all anxious to get to New Orleans after . . ." Abby shivered. "Ugh, I need a shower."

Dan sat silently in the back, wishing he knew the right thing to say to make everything okay again. But all he could think about was Micah's message.

While they unpacked the car, Dan could feel Jordan's eyes boring holes into the back of his head. He owed them both an explanation, he knew, but where to start? He hated to scare them any more tonight, especially before they went to sleep in a tent.

He wasn't even sure if his friends would believe what he had to say. He had never been completely up front with them about his ability to *see* things. There'd been a time last year when the stress had left them all seeing and hearing things that weren't quite there, but that was nothing like what Dan had come to think of as his power. He hadn't just seen echoes of the past as visions—Dan had lived them, even interacted with them.

And if Dan didn't come clean to his friends during this trip, he might never get another chance.

Under the glow of floodlights from the parking lot, they set to work putting up their tent, a job that Abby delegated expertly. Dan hammered the stakes into the moist ground a little harder

than was strictly necessary, but it felt good to hit something. In just over half an hour, the tent was as finished as it was ever going to be.

"Are you okay?" Abby asked, watching Dan unroll his sleeping bag. "You were hammering pretty hard there."

"I'm fine," he said, shrugging off the question.

"You're obviously not."

He didn't know what to say, and he hesitated just a bit too long.

"Fine, you know what? Don't tell me."

Abby climbed into her sleeping bag, still in her clothes. Last night she'd used one of the campground port-a-potties to change into pajamas, but tonight Dan suspected her anger was at least partly to mask her fear.

"I know you're ticked, Abby," Dan said, lighting one of their Coleman lamps and sitting cross-legged on his bedding. A light gust of wind rattled the tent fabric, and distant campers laughed, one of them howling loudly at the moon.

"It's not even a full moon," Abby grumbled, turning onto her side and away from Dan. Jordan gave him an encouraging look, though of course he knew only a small piece of what he was encouraging.

"Just let me explain, okay?" Dan sighed and closed his eyes, trying to figure out the best way to put this. "You're right. I'm not fine. There's . . . Look, I want this trip to be fun, okay? I really do, and I wouldn't spoil it for no reason. It's been amazing so far. Being with you two is . . . Well, it's the most fun I've ever had. I didn't want to bring anything up that would ruin the mood."

"So don't," she said woodenly.

"Hear him out," Jordan said.

With a big, huffing sigh, Abby turned over, just her eyes and hair visible above the lip of the forest-green sleeping bag. "Fine. I'm hearing you out. Explain."

Dan twisted and reached for his backpack, removing the thin, faded folder that held basically all he knew about his parents.

"Okay, well, part one is—I found something," he said, pulling out the pile of papers with shaking fingers. He handed it across to Jordan, and Abby wriggled out of her sleeping bag enough to read over his shoulder. "That was all in Professor Reyes's files. I went over everything in there with a fine-tooth comb, obviously, but there wasn't much."

Abby pushed her dark, feathery hair away from her face, squinting to read the police report on Dan's dad. She froze.

"Is this . . . is this your father? God. I had no idea, Dan."

"Neither did Jordan until I mentioned something at dinner," Dan murmured. Abby had taken the papers from him and began reading everything carefully. Jordan didn't try to stop her.

Abby picked up the postcard, the brief contents of which Dan had memorized months ago. The sepia-toned picture showed a looming brick building—one that wouldn't have been out of place on New Hampshire College's campus. The only parts of the address left were "HIGH STREET" and a city that looked like *ingt n* or *lington*, and there was a message written in pencil that had been mostly worn away, too.

love you very

risk, but there is always

love you very
risk, but there is always

HIGH STREET

ington

Dan's fingers clamped down hard on the postcard as he pulled it carefully out of Abby's hands. He wanted to believe that this was his mother's handwriting, and that maybe this postcard had been meant for him—that his parents had *had* to go. That he wasn't an accident or an afterthought.

A tight, cold feeling settled over his chest. Nine months after finding all this, Dan still wanted to know more. He looked at the front of the postcard again, running his fingertips lightly over the image. Someone had scribbled across the picture, but it was gibberish.

Abby had moved on to the heavily creased and stained map—a foldout road map of the United States, printed in 1990. A thin black line had been drawn in pen from New Orleans to Alabama, then Missouri, then up to Chicago, and finally to Pittsburgh.

The site of that little dot where the line ended jarred him. His town. His city. The year, 1990, wasn't so far off from when he was born in 1996. In the story he'd constructed based on the evidence, his parents had been criminals on the run. That's why they'd left him. Dan tensed, closing his eyes and wishing he had never found the folder in the first place.

"Dan . . ."

The tone in her voice was one of discovery, but right at this moment, he didn't care if Abby *had* noticed something he hadn't, he just wanted to be quiet and forget—to find a way to let go of his frustration before it sabotaged the trip.

"What?" he forced out.

"There's something on the back of this map," she said.

"I know."

Dan watched as they both looked at the message, handwritten in black marker and double-underlined.

<u>FIND THEM</u>

"So you think Professor Reyes wrote this? I still don't understand what she wanted with your parents," Jordan said, frowning and studying the map.

"She didn't want them, necessarily. She just wanted a living member of the warden's bloodline," he said. "I guess I was easier to find. Hell, I practically fell into her lap last summer."

He watched his friends share a look, and he answered before the questions started pouring out.

"So that's part two. I know we've joked about it in the past—how the weird connection between me and the warden went a little beyond your usual great-uncle–great-nephew relationship. But what I never told you guys is that Professor Reyes was after me because she thought I could see things from the past. Like, things related to the warden."

Silence.

Then, finally, Jordan asked, "And . . . can you?"

"Sometimes, yes." There was really no sugarcoating it. "I don't know what brings it on; it's not something I can control. Last summer I would get these waking dreams, almost like I was seeing things from the past through the warden's eyes. At the time I thought it was part of my disorder somehow. But then at Halloween, I saw things the warden couldn't possibly have seen."

Abby drummed her fingers on top of the family tree, looking as if she was thinking very carefully about how to respond.

When she spoke, it was not the reaction Dan was expecting. "Is this why you applied to NHCP to begin with? To find out about your family? It's not like I can throw stones—I was there looking for my aunt. But since we're being honest, I have to say, ever since you told us about being related to the warden, I've wondered if you didn't go *looking* for him last summer—if these visions you're talking about weren't part of some plan to bring him back."

"What? No! I swear to both of you, I didn't know anything about the warden or my parents when I first got to NHC," Dan insisted. "I don't know if it was coincidence or fate that brought me to Brookline last summer, but I was there, and I just . . . I don't want to get to a place ever again where I'm keeping secrets from you guys because I'm scared, okay? So there's something else I need to tell you. The third and final part."

He pulled out his phone and quickly brought up the message, shuddering when he found it was still there in his inbox. A part of him had been convinced it would be gone the next time he went looking.

"Here," he said. "Look at this."

"Holy shit," Jordan whispered, almost dropping Dan's phone when he glimpsed the message. "That's messed up."

"I think I saw Micah, too, just before we left NHC. It was so quick; I hoped it was my mind playing tricks. I hoped it was over."

Abby leaned across to make use of the lamp, taking the phone from Jordan and gasping. "But how is this possible? I thought they locked down accounts of . . . of those who have passed."

Dan could tell she was about to say "of dead people" but felt it was too harsh. Harsh or not, it was the truth.

Abby hugged her knees to her chest. "Unless you're saying you think this has something to do with your visions? But then how could we see it, too?"

"Exactly. It has to be a prank, right?" Dan asked, maybe emphasizing that desperate little *right* too much.

"It certainly could be," Abby said sternly. She couldn't take her eyes away from the phone. "Someone's sick idea of a joke."

"It's like the cloud or whatever," Jordan chimed in, nodding. "You can hack anything these days."

"God, Dan, this is a lot to handle." Abby pushed the phone away, finally looking up to meet his eyes. "Part of me can't believe this is really happening."

He gave them a wobbly smile. "Business as usual, I guess."

"It shouldn't be," Jordan replied, clapping him on the back. "I think you should message that person back and tell them to knock it off. Or report it! There has to be a way to get it taken care of."

He wasn't even touching the rest of what Dan had said, and Dan knew that was Jordan's way of saying it was fine. He'd moved on to solutions, always the problem solver.

"Jordan is right," Abby said, matching Dan's flimsy smile. "Report it. Then I bet the messages will stop."

"Yeah, obviously," Dan echoed. "I'll just report it." He picked up his phone, stowing it in his backpack before reaching to turn out the light. "Then the messages will stop."

Chapter
6

he monotony of the Alabama countryside was almost a welcome departure from the previous night's excitement. Dan stared out at the green and yellow pastures that unfolded around them, split up only occasionally by sudden strips of forest. Tiny farms dotted the horizon here and there, small enough to look like little Monopoly houses, too distant to look like real homes.

None of them had much to say this morning. Dan opened a Wi-Fi hotspot with his phone, and Abby propped Jordan's laptop open on her legs, humming along to Jordan's electronica while checking the route for where they were stopping next. The sound of her typing was soothing, almost like raindrops on a window, and Dan cuddled up to the side of the car, ready for a nap even though he'd hardly been awake two hours. Sleeping on the ground for two nights in a row hadn't exactly done great things for his back.

He was just about to drift off when Abby's voice broke in from up front.

"Check it out," she called, pointing at the laptop screen. "I think I've found something."

"I can't exactly look right now," Jordan said. "Describe it for me?"

Abby propped the laptop up on the center console and swiveled it to face Dan.

"Look familiar?" she asked, clearly pleased with herself. Okay, but she had a reason to be, Dan thought, blinking in shock at the image on the screen. It was the now-very-familiar building from the postcard, only in color this time.

"That's . . . How did you do that?"

"It wasn't that hard, really," she explained, tucking a piece of hair behind her ear. "The building in that photo was obviously either a hospital or a school, and I figured it had to be at least a little famous to be on a postcard. The letter in the caption looked more like an *l* than an *h*, so I figured it had to be Arlington and not Washington. At first I thought maybe it was an old hospital in Arlington, Virginia. But that wasn't leading to any matches, so finally I tried searching for 'Arlington school,' and this was on the first page of results. It's in Bessemer. Right near Birmingham."

"Wait—you're telling me that school is in Alabama?" Dan felt a chill running up his arm. He could hardly believe it. He scrolled down past the picture to the caption underneath. *Arlington School. Built in 1908, abandoned in the 1980s.*

"It's not even that far," Abby said. "We'd have to backtrack a little, but only two hours or so."

"Are you absolutely sure that's a good idea?" Jordan said. "I mean, no offense, Dan, but we don't exactly have a good track record when it comes to digging around in the past. And I for one find this coincidence a little freaky."

Dan tried to keep the urgency out of his voice as he said, "I mean, *I* would like to head back and see this place, yeah. But only if that's okay with you . . ."

Jordan looked at him in the rearview mirror, then looked over at Abby, who was one step shy of batting her eyelashes.

"Well, it doesn't seem like Uncle Steve is too concerned about when we get there," Jordan said. "Heck, the only person who misses me is my guild leader, Elanora, who keeps texting wanting to know when I'll be back for the raids. . . . All right, fine."

"Awesome, thank you," Dan said, no longer even the least bit sleepy. This was a break. This was a clue. He had given up thinking he would find anything new on his father and now this. . . . "It must have meant something to my parents, right? Why else would they have a postcard of some dinky old school? I want to see this place in person."

"Uh-oh—looks like there's one small problem." Abby grimaced, rubbing the back of her neck and reading farther down the page. "They've started demolishing the building this summer. There might not be much of it left to see."

"Then I guess Jordan better step on it."

メ メ メ メ メ メ

The school stood empty and watchful, a chain-link fence doing little to keep out the vandals that had ransacked the place. The vacant windows were streaked with bird droppings and graffiti. It was hard to imagine the place had ever been filled with students.

A wide brick staircase led up to the main entrance, and a tumble of broken furniture and junk formed a landslide down to the street level. All three of them leaned against the car, staring up at the school.

Dan held up the postcard, comparing the school in its prime to its now-dilapidated state.

"I can see why they're going to demolish it," Abby said softly. "I'm just glad we managed to get here with daylight to burn."

"It doesn't look safe to go inside." Jordan stared down the block, studying the various approaches to the doors. No matter what route they took, it would involve trespassing. "I'm not sure where we'd even begin."

But now Jordan was back in problem-solving mode. He pushed away from the car and drifted up the sidewalk. "Maybe there's a caretaker we can talk to. I'd really rather not go exploring and get shanked by hobos."

Up the hill, standing on the overgrown, weed-choked walkway, was a tall man, dressed in a rugged canvas jacket and jeans. "Like him," Dan said, picking his way over to a gap in the fence.

"Like who?" Jordan asked.

"Hey!" Dan shouted. The man seemed not to hear him, continuing across the school's littered courtyard and then disappearing around a corner. "Hey, do you take care of this place?"

Dan ran to keep up, stumbling over tumbled stones and the broken-up desks and chairs mounded in a sharp, nail-studded obstacle course that led all the way to the boarded-up door. Dan glimpsed the man again, this time slipping around the left corner of the school. The man wasn't running, and Dan easily caught up, flying around the corner and colliding with the stranger.

Or he *would* have collided with him, if he hadn't skidded right through him. Dan froze, feeling a cold wave of fright shiver down to his toes, a cold that persisted as the man backtracked and passed one more time through Dan's physical form. Keeping pace with the vision, Dan looked up into the man's face, seeing traces of his own nose, mouth, chin. . . . Was it possible? Was he really looking at . . .

"Dad?"

Dan really didn't want this to be his father. In all his previous visions, he'd only ever seen people who were already dead.

Not that he'd really held out hope of finding Marcus alive, but to have it confirmed like this nearly paralyzed him with terror all over again. Still, he followed as the ghostly man led him to a maintenance door around the back of the building. His father passed right through, leaving Dan to duck and weave through a few poorly nailed boards covering the doorway.

His shirt snagged on one of the jagged edges of the four-by-fours, but he ignored it, hurrying to follow his father deeper into the school. Marcus's clothes were out of fashion, or at least shabby, and Dan wondered *when* he was seeing—what time in his father's life this imprint belonged to. The inside of the school was a bigger mess than the outside, but that seemed to have been the case in Marcus's time, too, as he carefully dodged pieces of wall that had caved in and blocked certain corridors. He led Dan through to the moldering front entrance hall, where a pigeon dive-bombed for Dan's head and made him shout in alarm.

"You okay? Dan! Where did you go?" Abby's shout echoed through the collapsed innards of the school.

"I'm fine! I'll be out in a minute," he called back. At least he hoped that would be the case. The mold and bird droppings mingled to make an overpowering smell, and he grabbed his shirt and lifted the collar, burying his nose in the fabric to keep from gagging.

Blistering paint peeled in long coils from the walls and ceiling. Dan's father ducked through a sagging doorway and into what looked like a classroom beyond. Inside, he opened a closet door covered in graffiti.

"We can't stay," Marcus said to nobody. "Just leave it. This place is such a disaster, and we don't have time to pack everything. Do you really want to get caught here, Evie? Let's go."

He glanced over his shoulder in alarm, directly into Dan's face.

And then he was gone.

Chapter 7

*D*an stared into the dank bowels of the classroom storage closet. The shelves had been knocked out and scattered into the room, leaving a kind of cave for vagrants. A few pillows and blankets littered the floor, eaten to tatters by rodents and insects. He squeezed his nose shut with his thumb and forefinger, pressing into the closet and kneeling, searching among the disintegrating remnants of a camp. There was no telling how long it had been since the place was last used.

He toed aside the pillows and blankets. Something moved among the discarded bedding, distorting the fabric before tearing through it. A whip-thin rat darted out at him, shrieking and then scurrying out of the closet. Dan sank back against the gutted shelves, holding his chest and catching his breath from the sudden shock. The hole left by the rat showed a glimpse of faded yellow, and Dan carefully moved the blankets to find a sort of nest, torn pieces of paper piled together. Most of it had been chewed and soiled beyond recognition, but a few half sheets of paper still held visible text.

Dan gathered what he could, shuddering from the damp, foul smell and clumps of fur and droppings that clung to the pages. He poked around the closet for more, but there was nothing. Behind him, the school echoed with the voices and footsteps of his friends.

Out in the main hall, he discovered Abby documenting the ruins with her camera. Jordan hugged himself, staring around at the precariously open and broken ceiling.

"There you are," he said, breathing through his mouth. "Where the hell did you go?"

"I saw something," Dan said. "It might have been . . . I'm not sure. But there was some old junk in a closet. I took it to look at later."

"Dan," Abby said, staring at him over the eye of her camera. "What did you see?"

"One of those visions," he admitted. "I think it might have been my dad. Hopefully some of this stuff was theirs." Grimacing, he held up the stained, old pages.

"Delightful," Jordan mumbled, holding his nose and scowling at Dan like he was crazy.

"We could try and dry them out with my blow dryer," Abby suggested, unfazed. She returned to her camera, wandering over to a mound of rotting and piled tabletops. Her camera clicked softly as she shot the ceiling, the classrooms, Jordan. She was taking so many pictures that it was a few minutes before Dan noticed it, staring past her to the maintenance door he had entered through.

A softer, faster *click-click-click* came from the bushes right outside the door.

Abby wasn't the only one taking photos.

"What the hell," he whispered, racing toward the door.

A slim shadow huddled against the shrubs outside, photographing them. When Dan neared the door, the guy swung the camera over his shoulder on a strap and raced out of view.

Dan followed, cursing the low-hanging boards nailed over the maintenance hatch.

The guy was fast, far faster than Dan, nimbly leaping over the landslide of junk in the front yard. Skidding down the embankment, he reached a black motorcycle parked across the street from Abby's car. Out of breath, Dan stumbled down the hill, watching as the stranger hopped on the bike, slammed one foot down on the gas, and then executed a neat circle before speeding away. A red insignia flashed on the back of the cyclist's jacket, but Dan was too far away to read it, and he had missed the license plate, too.

Panting, Dan stared after the motorcycle as it disappeared.

"What was that?" Jordan was out of breath, too, running back toward him. "Did a cop see us?"

"I don't think it was a cop," Dan said. "Someone was photographing us. *Watching* us."

Chapter 8

$\mathcal{D}$an was tired of losing his appetite just before every meal rolled around.

"You really think this person was taking pictures of us?" Abby asked, leaning toward him with both elbows propped on the booth table. "Why would anyone bother?"

Two hours on the road had brought them back to the Montgomery area for a late lunch. They'd stopped in another diner to stretch and use the restroom, but none of them wanted to stay still for very long.

"I have no idea," Dan said. The whole drive here, he'd been trying to make sense of the vision in the school and the stranger photographing them. At least Abby and Jordan had heard the motorcycle, so Dan knew the encounter hadn't *all* been in his head. And on the bright side, Facebook had been indifferent enough to send a "We're looking into it" response to Dan's report of the incident.

"Hey, you love taking pictures of old crap, Abby. Maybe this weirdo likes taking pictures of people taking pictures of old crap," Jordan said, but he looked pale, nervous.

Dan didn't like it either.

"Well, whoever it was is probably still back in Birmingham," Abby pointed out, "but we should keep our eyes open anyway."

"Agreed," Dan said. He had only managed to order a soda, and was sipping it slowly while nibbling on the complimentary bread. He never liked taking his meds on an empty stomach, and the snacking helped.

"Once we pass Mobile we'll be coming up on the Magnolia Cemetery," Abby said, switching tracks and trying, and failing, to lighten the mood. "If we're still okay with stopping, I've been dying to see this place."

"Phrasing?" Jordan said wryly.

"Okay, *excited* to see it," Abby said, sticking out her tongue. "Mr. Blaise wouldn't shut up about it. I think he did some charcoal sketches of it back when he was our age."

Their waitress, Randy, appeared just then, snapping her gum and bringing them the check. She had candy-apple red hair permed out in a frizzy halo that wouldn't look out of place on Ronald McDonald's sister. "Magnolia, you said? Y'all really should see it if you're not in a big hurry. I suppose it ain't normal to recommend a cemetery to tourists, but this one's special."

"Yes! Have you been?" Abby directed her attention fully to Randy. "I've been looking into these rum runners from the time of Prohibition and the history of them is so, so cool. I'm trying to find a way to add them into this photo project I'm working on."

Dan twisted to stare out the window at the car, where the damp old pages he had found were drying in the sun on top of the Neon.

"If you two want to give me money for the check, I'll be right out," Abby said shortly, turning back to finish her conversation with Randy. Dan hated that they were fighting already, even a little bit, but he truly was anxious to see what was in those papers.

"So, you really think you saw your dad?" Jordan asked as they walked to the car. "I mean, your *real* dad. Wait, is that kosher? Is it weird to say *real*? Sandy and Paul are great. You know I think they're totally great."

"No offense taken," Dan assured him truthfully. He didn't exactly know what the correct nomenclature was himself. "I think it might have been him. I mean, he looked like me. Didn't sound much like me, but that's not so strange. I heard him talking to someone—'Evie,' he said—but she didn't appear to me."

Jordan nodded, chewing thoughtfully on the bendy straw in his to-go cup. His eyes darkened behind his thick-rimmed glasses. "If you did see him, what do you suppose he was doing in that old school?"

"Squatting, maybe?" Dan suggested. "It sounded like he was in a hurry, maybe even being chased. I'm hoping in the rush to get out, he and my mom might have left something behind."

"There's only one way to find out."

✗✗✗✗✗✗

The pages crinkled and cracked in his hands.

Abby and Jordan remained silent, but he could feel the combined weight of their anticipation bearing down on him like a concrete block. They didn't want the smelly, moldy papers in the car any longer than they needed them, so the three of them stood in a semicircle in the parking lot.

"Okay," Dan said on an inhalation. "Here goes. What do you have for me, Mom and Dad?"

Breathing through his mouth, he pulled the top page close and squinted at the faded handwriting. It was a letter addressed to *Marc & Evie*.

"'I hope you two are safe,'" Dan read aloud, making out the writing as best he could. "'A PO box is smart, but still traceable. Just lay low until this stuff with Trax Corp. blows over. They're leaning on me hard to give up my sources, but those morons know I won't budge. Some of their people have come sniffing around the office. Thugs. The animal cruelty was a big find, but the smuggling is even bigger. I'll try to keep that bloodsucker Tilton off your backs. Just don't stay in one place for too long, all right? In a few months Trax will have more to worry about than a few trespassers and you can come back to town. Everything is fine at the *Whistle*. You know me, I can hold down a fort.'" Lowering the pages, Dan let Abby take them to inspect. "It's signed 'Maisie.'"

"It sounds like your parents were whistleblowers or something," Abby said, reading the page over again. She flipped to the second salvaged sheet. "Another letter from that Maisie person. Sounds like whatever your parents found, it got this Trax Corp. shut down."

Dan went to her side, reading over her shoulder.

"And there was a warrant out for their arrest," Dan added, pointing. "Even before the police report I have. I guess the breaking and entering wasn't an isolated incident."

"But your parents must have been right," Jordan said, going back to his phone. "I mean, Trax Corp. closed, yeah? So they must have been doing something illegal."

Dan nodded, but he was elsewhere, imagining how frightening it must have been for his parents to move from place to place, dodging arrest. They must have been squatting in the school, avoiding motels or any places where they might be recognized. He couldn't believe his own parents were *fugitives*. Of course, after bouncing around from one foster family to the next throughout his childhood, the revelation felt right, somehow. As much as he loved and appreciated Paul and Sandy, there had always been a noticeable but unmentioned gulf between their all-American goodness and his darker tendencies.

"There must be more about this company online," Dan mused. "If they got shut down, there might be articles about it. Although this was in the eighties. If it wasn't a big company, there might not be much."

"Maybe not," Jordan said, hunched over his phone. "But it looks like the *Whistle* was definitely a newspaper. Small one, but they've got a Wikipedia entry. Maisie Moore was the editor-in-chief until 1995. No mention of your parents, but the paper was based in Metairie. That's not far from New Orleans. Maybe Maisie still lives in the area."

"That's brilliant," Abby said. She handed the letters back to Dan carefully, mindful of their delicate state. "She knew your parents, Dan. We can look her up when we get to town."

"Don't get my hopes up." But they were already up. What if Maisie Moore had contact information on file for his parents? After all these years of not knowing, could finding them be as easy as that?

Chapter
9

"*A*re you sure it's okay?"

"Honestly, Abby, it's fine. I know how much you've been looking forward to seeing this cemetery. I'm not going to ruin it for you."

And anyway, they were already parked on a narrow street nearby. Dan could hardly remember the drive. He was functioning in the strictest sense of the word, but even simple things like fastening his seat belt had taken extraordinary effort. When they'd made a quick stop for gas, Jordan had insisted on paying the bill, since Dan couldn't find his wallet.

Abby opened his car door, and he tumbled out onto the sidewalk, blinking up at the overcast sky as if he had just woken from a long, restless sleep. The enormous cemetery was protected by a spindly wrought-iron gate. He and Jordan followed Abby down the sidewalk to the entrance, passing below a sloped sign with *Magnolia Cemetery* worked into the metal.

Jordan shuddered. "I hate cemeteries. I never feel like I should be in one, you know? Like unless you are literally a dead person or there to bring flowers, you should stay far away."

"Yeah, Abby might owe us a round of milk shakes later."

She'd been right about the architecture, though—gorgeous, sprawling monuments that could house a person or a small

family of pets popped up every few feet along the path. The three of them wandered from the main walkway and onto the short-cropped lawn. Dan was careful not to tread even close to any of the flat gravestones sinking into the ground.

"Are you sure we're just browsing? You seem like a woman on a mission," Jordan called to Abby, who strode ahead confidently.

"Randy gave me some directions."

"Who?" Jordan cried.

"Randy. Randy, our waitress? Right, you weren't paying attention. She told me about some monuments to check out. I jotted down the directions. Just follow me."

Neither of them protested.

"So this project of yours," Dan said, making conversation to fill the heavy, empty air of the cemetery. "Is this something you're going to show to your new professors or what?"

She shrugged, chewing on her lower lip as they picked their way around the gravestones. "Actually, it's . . . I've just been thinking. A lot. Maybe too much." With a sigh, she paused to snap a few pictures of trees towering above them. "There's been so much pressure to pick a school and do the right thing, the *expected* thing, and I'm not sure that's what I want anymore."

"I guess your dad was pretty tough on you about applications," Dan said.

"Feral, I think, is the better word." She laughed, bitterly. "This is what I like," she said, gesturing to the camera and then the open air. "I'm just not sure spending a whole crapload of money to get an art degree is the smartest choice. Plenty of artists do fine without it. And I'm guaranteed to be poor right after graduating anyway, so why make myself even poorer? It's

not like I want to get a degree to teach art, I want to be *living* it."

"So what are you saying?"

"I'm saying I at least want to take a year off." She might have started hesitantly, but now she spoke with conviction. "At first, my parents said they wouldn't support me if I didn't go to college, but then finally they said if I could show them how I would use the year, they'd consider it. And who knows, maybe if this project is good enough, I can get it in a gallery back home or something."

Dan nodded dumbly. After everything, she still hadn't felt comfortable telling him something as big as this?

"Anyway, so what if my parents don't support me? Jordan's parents aren't supporting him and he's surviving."

"And thriving," Jordan said, but it sounded sarcastic to Dan's ears.

Dan just tried to keep up, watching the names of the dead roll past him. A high-pitched wind whined through the open field, cutting through the warmth of the day like a knife. It sounded like a shriek. Jordan had been right before; they didn't belong there. It didn't matter how many colorful bouquets were heaped on the tombs and the steps of the grand mausoleums—it took only one rotting lump of flowers by his feet to remind Dan of the thousands of dead under and around them.

"Jesus, nobody does spirits like the South," Jordan whispered. "You go to a cemetery back home and it's like, eh, whatever— creepy, I guess, but not like this. It just feels like the dead are *angrier* here."

Dan nodded. "I'm just crossing my fingers that I don't have any visions in this place."

"Yikes." Jordan blanched. "I didn't even think of that."

Abby led them to a far corner of the cemetery, where the graves were less impressive. Most were simply rough-hewn rocks wedged into the dirt and scratched with initials and years. But beyond that smattering of markers rose a single monument, a stepped limestone monstrosity that seemed to lord over the lesser stones. A snarling face had been chiseled into the monument, grotesque and exaggerated, as if a demon were caught inside and had pressed and pressed against the stone until it stretched tight over its face like ivory fabric.

A single tree, half-withered and racing the monument toward the overcast sky, grew from the very corner of the fenced property. It hung over them, oddly still in the wind.

"This is it!" Abby said excitedly, getting out her camera and snapping photos.

JAMES CONLEN ORSINI 1894–1935
'Ambition's debt is paid.'
Je ne te quitterai point que je ne t'aie vu pendu

"I will not leave until I have seen you hanged," Jordan read. Abby and Dan turned in unison to glance at him. "What? I took three years of French, might as well use it."

"This guy sounds like a real riot," Dan muttered.

"Don't look so surprised," Abby teased from behind her camera. He listened to the soft rush of the shutter as it clicked in between her words. "He was a criminal, a gangster, not exactly the kind of

guy to go quietly in his sleep. He died in a shootout after a bunch of his buddies sprang him out of lockup to avoid execution."

"And you're sure you want to photograph his grave? You're not afraid of catching his spirit or something?" Jordan asked, poking nervously at the stud in his lip with his tongue.

"Stop fiddling with that thing, it's going to get infected."

"You're going to get infected."

"Very original, Jordan."

Dan couldn't look at that hideous face on the monument anymore. He wandered around to the back of the statue, kicking at the overgrown grass. The groundskeepers apparently didn't care so much about this corner of the cemetery, letting clumps of weeds and dry leaves gather. Nobody had come to leave flowers recently. Dan kept circling the statue, coming to a halt just before he fell face-first into a hole.

One of the gravestones had been overturned and pushed aside, and a messy hole had been dug in front of it. There didn't seem to be anything inside except for a few worms and chunks of fallen sod.

"Hey, guys," Dan called, peering over the edge and down into the hole. He was going to invite them over to see the weird, open grave, but then he stopped, noticing a smudge of white in the dirt. Kneeling down, he carefully brushed aside the loose dirt and pebbles, revealing what he first thought might be the jaw of a dog or small animal. His fingers hovered over its faded surface, a sudden desire to *pick it up, hold it, never let it go* taking hold of him and squeezing. He swayed a little, then caught himself and backed away. Dan stared at the odd little curved bone. It wasn't from a dog, he realized with a lurch in his stomach, but from a human child.

Abby appeared around the statue, snapping photos as she went.

"Ew, gross," Jordan said, catching sight of the open grave. "Don't tell me there's a body in there."

"Nope, just a single bone," Dan said. "From a *kid*. It looks like someone carved things into it."

"Oh, God," Abby murmured, but she raised her camera and took a photo of it, then stopped, a strange, distant light coming into her eyes. "I shouldn't have done that," she said, holding her camera near her waist. "I don't know why I did that, but I shouldn't have. I'm going to delete it."

"Does anyone else get a weird feeling from it?" Dan asked.

"It's a kid's jawbone, of course I get a weird feeling from it!" Jordan refused to look at the hole. He started to walk back in the direction of the car. The wan light shifted over the tree and Orsini's monument, leaving Abby and Dan in a cooler swath of shadow.

"We should cover it up," Abby whispered. They shared a long look, neither of them moving nearer to the thing. Finally, Dan relented, shuffling closer and using his shoe to nudge dirt back over the bone. He glanced at it one last time, noticing that a string had been tied around one end. He didn't want to know what that was for.

Dan heard the quiet snap of a camera shutter and frowned.

"I thought you weren't going to photograph it," he said, covering the bone completely.

"I'm not," Abby replied. And she wasn't.

Dan spun, tracking the soft noise to a clump of flowering bushes back the way they had come. He didn't hesitate, tearing off toward the figure kneeling next to the bush. He was dressed head to toe in black again, slender and athletically built. Actually, up close, Dan couldn't even tell if he was chasing a man or a woman.

It didn't matter. This time he would catch the bastard. He sprinted, narrowly dodging headstones, his lungs burning as he tried to keep up. The path back to the gate was vaguely familiar, but this stranger was fast. . . . Too fast. Dan persisted, hoping to at least catch a license plate or a better look at the motorcycle. It was the same person from the school—that much he knew for sure.

He couldn't keep up. Still he pounded across the cemetery, hearing Abby call after him as his target grew farther and farther away until he or she disappeared around the trees and hedgerows that flanked the cemetery gates.

"Damn it," he seethed, skidding onto the pebbly path that emptied out onto the street. He gulped down breaths, glancing left and right. The motorcycle was parked not far from Abby's car, and Dan mustered a few more jogging steps, but the guy was already gunning the engine and swerving out into the street.

Dan ran the last of the way leaning over, hands on his knees, catching his breath and staring down at a thick tire tread.

"Did you see them?" Abby had caught up and Jordan wasn't far behind. He heard their footsteps as they ran up to meet him.

"No," he muttered. "They were wearing that damn helmet the whole time." He lifted his head and swallowed a lump. "I think it's pretty clear, though. We're being followed."

Chapter 10

The pain was a whisper, dull and annoying, like a voice coming in from another room. He almost wanted more of it, wanted the voice to be louder. At least if he could figure out where he hurt, then he might be able to fix it.

Dan twisted, flailed, but he was caught. He couldn't do this again—he couldn't be that vulnerable, caught, and outsmarted. First the Sculptor—no, Felix—and then Professor Reyes. He had to escape this time.

His first wish was granted. Pain roared through his hand, his arm, his shoulder, so acute and terrible it burned behind his eyes. Then his eyes opened and he came awake, lurching up out of his seat with a drowned man's gasp.

"Everything okay? You fell asleep." Abby glanced over at him from the driver's seat.

Dan grappled for understanding. Right. The cemetery, then a quick drive-through dinner. Now they were sailing through the night, and the last traces of metropolitan comfort were gone. They were so far south he wouldn't be surprised to roll down the window and taste salt air.

"Dan?"

"I just had a weird dream," he said, rubbing a hand over the patchy growth of whiskers on his face. He still couldn't manage to grow even a half-assed goatee. "Where are we? I thought we were only a few hours from New Orleans?"

"Well, we *are* still only a few hours from New Orleans, but here's the thing. There's this library I really wanted to see. It's the last stop I want to make before Uncle Steve's, I swear." Her brows lifted, one half of her mouth curving up in what he knew was a hopeful, testing smile.

"What did Jordan say?"

It was then that Dan noticed Jordan snoring softly in the backseat, his music audible from the headphones slung around his neck.

"I wouldn't ask," Abby said quickly, lowering her voice, "because I know Jordan is excited to see his uncle and move in, and we're all ready to sleep in beds again, but they've got a whole box of stuff that belonged to Jimmy Orsini. It's incredible it even survived."

"Him again?" Dan took a lukewarm soda out of the cup holder near his knee and took a swig. "Abby, do you really think telling the definitive history of some gangster guy is going to make things right with your parents?"

He saw her stiffen at the cavalier way he described—or *attempted* to describe—her art.

Abby relaxed her grip on the wheel a little, taking a deep breath. "It's more than that now. I'm genuinely interested in this. I mean, these local people, people like Orsini—everybody we've met has had some scary story or something about him, but where does that all come from? He's not like Bonnie and Clyde or Al Capone, where you can find all this stuff about him online. It's like he's a real urban legend or something. How does that kind of thing happen?"

"Good question," Dan said, yawning. "Yeah, maybe there's something there."

"It's okay, Dan, you don't have to pretend to be interested. Just let me make this last stop and then I'll try and shut up about it."

"I am interested, Abby, especially if you're going to take a year off to really work on this," he said. "It's a big deal for you. I mean, it's going to be your whole life soon, right?"

She nodded, smirking. "One day I'll educate you about all this stuff."

"Hey, I don't make you read Goethe, right? I can like something about you without understanding it," he said.

Dan sank down into the car seat, staring off at the road ahead. He smiled a little, glad at least that Abby and Jordan were there to cheer him up. It was impossible to imagine going through the surprises alone. Sometimes he was 100 percent certain they were meant to be a trio, that somehow, they'd find a way to stay close next year, even after their new lives took them away to new adventures, new goals.

"So where is this library, anyway?" Dan asked.

"It's in a city called Shreveport. It's closed for the night, so we'll have to pitch the tent again and go first thing in the morning."

Immediately, Dan wished he hadn't asked. He knew the name Shreveport. It was the last city where Micah had lived before going to New Hampshire. He'd never returned.

✗✗✗✗✗

Jordan had been confused to wake up in Shreveport instead of in New Orleans, but he'd gotten over it pretty quickly.

The city was beautiful, overlooking the Red River and teeming with culture—a welcome break from all the flat expanses they'd seen from the road. The library was in a neighborhood a few miles outside of the city proper, and the route took them past one historic mansion after another.

Abby consulted the phone in her lap, then handed it to Dan. "Mind navigating? It's already in the GPS."

"In a quarter mile," he said, mimicking the robotic voice of the GPS app, "turn left onto Shady Oak Road. Your destination will be on the right."

She laughed, slowing on a street filled with old shops and restaurants before following his directions. "That bakery on the corner looks cute. And oh, look! They have an ice-cream shop."

"It's nine in the morning."

"Never too early for ice cream," she said with an impish smile.

They turned into a parking lot the size of a Post-it note, stopping right up against another squat brick building. Only one other car was there, a red Chevy truck in decent condition.

"Jordan," Dan said, turning to poke his friend in the shin. "We're at the smallest library we've ever seen. You're coming inside to keep me company."

"Mmf. Can't I just stay in here and sleep?"

"No," he and Abby replied in strict unison.

The nearby bakery let off a tantalizing perfume of baking bread. That was enough to perk up Jordan, who was promised a doughnut if he managed to stay awake for the duration of the library trip. Dan and Jordan fell into step, letting Abby race ahead, a Starbucks latte from earlier firmly in hand.

Jordan's phone buzzed as they passed through the doors of the library and into a thick miasma of dust and old, wet paper smell.

"Well, I'll be damned," Jordan whispered. "That lady actually got back to me?"

"Who?" Dan asked absently. He gazed around at dozens of display cases, most of them showcasing Civil War weapons and uniforms. At least seventeen different Confederate flags fluttered down from the crossbeams of the ceiling. A cheerful young woman in a flannel shirt and denim skirt greeted Abby, lapsing into chitchat with her immediately. She had an adorable, Dolly Parton twang.

"The journalist, the one who wrote about your mom and dad? I did some Googling. She's not working for the *Whistle* anymore, but she's still in newspapers. I got her new email address from the *Metairie Daily* and told her we'd come across some old letters she wrote." Jordan paused to read the message on his phone. "She says she wants to see them, but she'll only meet in person."

"It's something," Dan said noncommittally, but his palms began to sweat. There was no denying it; he wanted to meet her as soon as possible. "We should set up a time to meet her when we get to town."

"Roger, I'll ask about her schedule."

"Will you two be okay if I head back to the archives for a few minutes?" Abby asked, waiting with the library worker next to the reception and intake desk. "I swear I won't be all day."

"We'll behave," Jordan promised.

Abby smirked and followed the girl down the corridor and through a pair of swinging doors. Two open archways led off in

opposite directions from reception. Dan drifted through the one on the right, hands in his pockets, his thoughts far away from the shelves upon shelves of musty-smelling books.

A few limp puppets spilled out of a crate in the corner, surrounded by low, child-sized bookcases filled with suitably colorful titles.

Dan went to the grimy window overlooking the parking lot. There was no sign of a motorcycle, just the quiet stretch of shops and one of the bakery assistants taking a smoke break on the back steps.

"Man, the South is messed up," Jordan muttered. Dan found his friend a few shelves away, perusing a glass-cased display of open photo albums and vintage books. "Like, what about that says fun to you? *Revelers Take to the Streets in New Orleans. . . .* I'm sorry, but I would not revel in an outfit like that. That is not an outfit for reveling."

Dan examined the photograph in question and its description, laughing quietly. The row of men in hoodies and primitive animal masks did, in fact, look less like a party and more like a horror show. He couldn't make out anything behind the eyes of their masks—rabbit, cat, pig, fox—and the dead stares of the animal faces seemed to follow him as he slid away from the case.

"What are you doing?" Dan said, noticing Jordan and checking to see that they weren't being watched. Carefully, Jordan had plucked at the brass latch on the display case. It wasn't locked, and the case swung open.

"Nobody's here, and anyway, I want to see if there are any pictures from around Uncle Steve's house. He lives right there in the city. He'd get a kick out of it."

At least Jordan had the sense to handle the old book gingerly, drawing it out and placing it down on the next case over. Jordan turned each page delicately, revealing more photographs of "revelers" in the animal masks. Dan watched the descriptions of the photos go by—*Jazz Festival on Bourbon Street Draws Record Crowd*; *Riverboat Runs Aground, Five Dead*; *Jimmy "Spats" Orsini to Hang on March 3* . . .

"Whoa, stop." Dan put his hand down on Jordan's, forcing him to go back a page. "Abby will want to see this."

"Good catch." After the briefest hesitation, Jordan tugged the newspaper clipping out of its little triangle clips, turning the pages back to what had originally been shown. "Nobody will miss this."

Dan hoped he was right. Framed photos on the walls watched them as surely as the hollow-eyed masks, Civil War soldiers staring out at them with blank eyes, as if sitting so long for the photographs had turned the men to stone.

Dan lifted the book to tuck it back in its case, and a few loose pages shuffled free as he did so, fluttering to the ground. Dan swore, kneeling to pick them up. Just more photos, he realized, and a slip or two of newsprint. One scrap was folded into a tight square. He stood and handed Jordan the loose pages to fit back into the book, but curiosity got the better of him. Unfolding the square, he found another headline Abby might want to see.

Two Witnesses in Orsini Trial Dead, One Missing

The headline was the only part of the article he could read; the rest of the story was obscured by what looked like a handwritten poem.

TWO WITNESSES IN ORSINI TRIAL DEAD, ONE MISSING

Be not too happy nor too proud

to suppress the testimony of two witnesses

Beware your hide, crow not too loud;

room Thursday.

The Bone Artist steals and then he leaves

a tenant on the Mt. Olive

Dan read it aloud, squinting to make out the messy handwriting.

Be not too happy nor too proud
Beware your luck, crow not too loud;
The Bone Artist steals and then he leaves:

The page had been torn across at the bottom, the rest of the poem lost to the ages.

"See what I mean about the South?" Jordan whispered, shaking his head. "What's the matter with these people?"

"I'm taking this for Abby, too," Dan said. "Maybe she'll know how to interpret it."

Chapter

11

"*I* don't know if I'm proud or disappointed that you stole this stuff for me." Abby swayed a little, clutching the bottle of white wine Jordan had convinced some guy to buy for them outside of a Kum & Go. She had the news clippings spread out on the tent floor before her, as well as the notes she had taken while viewing the collection of Orsini's possessions.

"You can always mail them back if you get a sudden attack of conscience," Jordan pointed out. He took the bottle from Abby, drinking deeply. "Now see, this is how I pictured this drop-off going. Merrymaking, you know?"

"Stealing from libraries and drinking ill-gotten booze?" Dan asked. He didn't feel like sharing in the wine, afraid it might make him emotional and less capable of holding back his eagerness to reach Maisie Moore. They could have been in New Orleans already, but Abby and Jordan had wanted to stay in Shreveport for the day and spend one more night in the tent.

Uncle Steve had been cool with this. But Paul and Sandy were anxious for Dan to be off the road. At least Abby was pleased.

"Yes! *Yes.* We're going to turn this trip around yet, you'll see," Jordan crowed, beaming at him over the shiny bottle mouth.

"Sorry for all the stops and the camping," Abby said. "You're saints for putting up with it. I think things will get a bit more exciting in *N'Awlins*. Or, well, hopefully the good kind of exciting."

"*If* we make it there," Dan couldn't help saying. He turned to Jordan. "Are you going to finish that before you pass out?"

Jordan hugged the bottle tightly to his chest. "Of course," he slurred. "I paid thirty American dollars for this crappy wine. I'm getting my money's worth!"

Thirty dollars, yes, although half of that had been the bribe that convinced the trucker to buy it for them in the first place.

"Just take it easy. You're up first driving tomorrow."

Groaning, Jordan recorked the bottle and stored it near their small cooler in the corner. "Damn you and your logic."

"Good night, Jordan." Dan rolled onto his side and then half-way down into his sleeping bag. Crickets and frogs chorused, a constant underlying chirp that sounded disconcertingly close. Dan was accustomed to hearing the same night music back home in Pittsburgh, but usually he had the benefit of a window and walls between him and the creepy crawlies.

He hadn't realized how exhausted he was until he woke up again, startled out of a light doze by the buzzing of his phone. Dan groped for his phone in the darkness, though it was hard to hear over Jordan's snores and the sound of singing crickets.

When he found it, Dan rubbed his eyes, jolted to greater alertness by the light of the screen. His skin felt drawn and itchy, tightness around his eyes signaling that he needed at least a few more hours to feel truly rested. But he was awake now, and he flicked the lock open on his screen. He stared down at the notification. Facebook. His gut clenched. Two in the morning. Nobody would be messaging him now, he knew that, and he knew what he would see when he opened the app. But he did it anyway.

Micah had written again, this message more direct than the last:

g et u p th
e watch e rs wi ll find
u

The watchers?

There was no time to reflect. Sudden pinpoints of light bounced along the taut wall of the tent. He shut off his phone, afraid to give off even the slightest glow. Somebody was coming. He recognized the up-and-down bounce of the flashlights moving in time with footsteps.

He clapped a hand over Jordan's snoring mouth, listening to the grass swish under two pairs of shoes. The yellow circles of light on the tent wall grew as the people got closer. Dan strained to hear their voices, his heart hammering up into his throat.

Get up. The watchers will find you.

How could the Micah impersonator know?

"We shouldn't be here," one voice was saying, a soft voice, almost sweet, maybe belonging to a young woman.

"I have to see," another voice responded. This one was low and decidedly masculine. "He might be my only shot."

Could they mean Dan? Or maybe Jordan? Dan felt his friend try to twist out of his grasp, but Dan couldn't let the snoring sabotage his eavesdropping.

"You can't sneak up on folk like this. It ain't right."

The masculine voice let out a sigh, and Dan watched the flash-light beams halt and then finally retreat. The voices grew softer, too, muddling with the hush of the grass as the strangers turned and left. "You're right. There's a better way."

So they weren't going to be ambushed and killed in the night—that was a plus. But Dan wasn't satisfied. He wanted to know who was following them. He carefully eased out of his sleeping bag and the tent, pocketing his phone to use as a light. He had to be quick, but also quiet. The last thing he wanted was to alert them to his presence.

What if they were armed? What if they abducted him? Jordan and Abby would wake up and think he had abandoned them in the night.

My parents were brave. I can be brave, too.

He followed the flashlight beams as they bounced along the ground. The campsite was mostly empty, just a field at the edge of a dense wood, barrels for trash cans and streetlights marking the boundaries of the dirt parking lot. Dan followed, low to the ground, then dashed for the cover of one of the tall, wide trash bins.

The beams showed little, but in the parking lot they shone over the wide hood of a red muscle car, a Mustang or a Charger or one of those. Abby was the one who knew cars—maybe she could figure it out from the description. The doors closed and the car pulled out without turning on its lights. There wasn't much in the way of moonlight, but now Dan could tell that it was definitely an old car.

His palms slipped down the side of the trash bin, slick with frightful sweat. He was being followed. Hunted. He wondered

if one of those two had been the motorcyclist, and why they had come to find them in the night only to leave without accomplishing anything.

Dan sighed and kicked at the grass, standing and making his way back to the tent.

Abby and Jordan were waiting for him outside, peering at him with groggy eyes.

"What's going on? Why were you smushing my face while I slept?" Jordan asked, pressing a yawn into the crook of his elbow.

"We had visitors," Dan said, trying to keep the tremor out of his voice. "Two. I woke up to another message from Micah. He said something about watchers finding me, and then immediately I heard someone approaching the tent."

Abby reached for Jordan's forearm, clutching it. *"What?"*

"I know," Dan said, glancing back at the parking lot. "I don't like it either. But I don't know. They didn't seem hostile. And they left right away—just went back to their car and took off."

"Okay, that's it, we are getting our asses to Steve's right now," Jordan said hoarsely. "I don't care how many speed limits I have to break. I'm fed up with drive-through food, I'm fed up with sleeping on the ground, and I am sure as shit fed up with being *followed*."

Jordan tossed up his hands and stomped back into the tent, gathering his sleeping bag in a frenzy.

But Abby lingered outside, nervously tugging at the edges of her shirt. "Dan . . ."

"Jordan's right. We'll be safer at Uncle Steve's. I don't like being out here in the open, and it's a five-hour drive to New Orleans."

She nodded, reaching out and touching his shoulder lightly. "Do you think this thing with Micah is, well, *real*? The timing just seems so strange for it to be someone pulling a prank. And if you really did have a vision at Arlington School . . ."

That unlikely and unpleasant thought had crossed his mind. "I have no idea. I just wish I knew how to stop it."

The moonlight grew muted, white light turning to silver and then gray as clouds settled in heavy clumps in the sky. Abby squeezed his shoulder, but in the darkness, he could barely see her as she ducked into the tent to collect her things.

He looked down at his phone again, staring as it lit up— another message indicator pulsing above the time, the weather, the date . . .

Biting down hard on his lower lip, Dan read the new message.

t urn ba
ck turn b a ck or be foun d
in t h e i r territory

Chapter

12

"Their territory? What the hell does that mean?" Jordan swerved dangerously, punctuating his questions with the beat of his fist on the wheel.

Dan watched the fields and trees of northern Louisiana give steady ground to the spindlier flora of the bayou, the trees oddly thin and anemic. Long spits of water came up alongside the road, then sometimes dashed under it as the pavement transitioned seamlessly into bridges and then back again.

Still flat, though. Still disgustingly humid.

His head stuck to the window as he tried to peel it away, and the sigh he gave glazed the glass in a tepid fog. "I don't know, Jordan. I've gone over it about a thousand times in my head and it's not getting me anywhere."

"Uncle Steve was in the Special Forces. He'll know what to do," Jordan said, but Dan didn't see how that solved anything.

"Plenty of retro cars around," Abby said from the backseat. She had decided to point out every single vintage car that drove up next to them or trailed behind. After a dozen or so of these alerts, Dan reminded her that he wasn't at all sure what make or model they were looking for. Abby was unperturbed. "Not seeing many black motorcycles," she said.

"Can we turn the AC up?" Dan groused.

Jordan's phone jingled merrily and he nodded toward Dan. "Check that, will you? I put a notification on new emails in case Maisie Moore gets back to me."

"Probably just your clan leader again," Dan muttered, but he picked up the phone anyway.

"*Guild* leader, and so what if it was? I am like ten Ultimates away from full one-eighties and that jerk Raptus isn't going to kill himself—"

"Holy crap," Dan said, sitting up straighter and silencing Jordan's rambling. "She wrote back. Hold on, let me see what she has to say."

Abby crawled up close to read over his shoulder. Her long dark hair brushed his arm as she leaned in.

"'Thanks for getting back to me so promptly. You can understand that with the personal nature of those letters I would prefer to discuss them face-to-face,'" Dan read. "'Every once in a while I think about Evie and Marcus and my heart just dies a little. They were two of the best I ever worked with, real journalists, real investigators, the kind you don't see in the click-bait age. But that's a discussion for another time.'" Dan took a deep breath. "'You said you know their kid? That's amazing. I'd love to meet him. I'm free most of this week for a lunch meeting.'" Dan paused. "You told her about me?"

"Why not? I thought it was a good angle to get her talking."

"Looks like it worked," Abby pointed out with a laugh.

"She actually *knew* them. I mean, it sounds like they were more than coworkers. I wonder if she knows. . . . Gah. I'm getting way ahead of myself," Dan said, staring down at the email, a little awestruck.

"Someone sounds excited," Abby said. She poked him lightly in the ear, giggling as he flinched away.

"I guess I am. I'd just like to know what happened to them, why they—" Dan cleared his throat, putting Jordan's phone back in the cup holder to charge. "Where they went."

But he had a gut feeling that *where* was not a place, but a state of being. Seeing his father in the school had all but confirmed their fates.

"Try not to be disappointed if she doesn't know all that much," Abby said softly. "It sounds like they haven't worked together in a very long time. There's a chance she lost track of them completely."

Dan nodded, wanting badly to take Abby's advice but feeling his hopes rise all the same. "And anyway, I'm not just here to meet Maisie Moore. We're here for Jordan. We're here to have fun in a whole new city. I'll have plenty to keep me busy," he said, forcing a smile. The alert on his phone signaled it was time to take his meds for the day. He fished the orange pill bottle out of his bag and noticed the *MARCUS DANIEL CRAWFORD* folder next to it.

His hopes had been raised and dashed and then raised again. He hoped this Maisie woman wouldn't be another dead end.

✗✗✗✗✗

"Are you sure that's not the ocean?" Dan pressed his nose flat to the window, staring out at the endless stretch of blue water. If he looked down, it made him dizzy, the glassy surface of the lake right there, just a sheer drop down from the bridge.

"Yup, I'm sure," Jordan said. "It's a lake. Wanted to bring you guys in this way even if it adds an extra thirty minutes. It's way more impressive to take the Pontchartrain Causeway."

Dan had never seen anything like it in his life, the causeway running over the lake in a clean white curve that subtly rose and rose, dark blue water surrounding them and stretching to the horizon. It felt like an alien world, like civilization had disappeared underneath an apocalyptic level of consuming water.

"My mom hates it," Jordan added. "Makes her feel claustrophobic."

"I can understand why." Abby sounded less than thrilled from the backseat. In the rearview mirror her complexion had taken on a green tint. "What happens if there's an accident? Or your car breaks down?"

"Do you really want to know?" Jordan asked.

"No."

Twenty visible miles of utter isolation. For the first time in days, Dan felt himself relax. Nobody could get to them here. Who would want to? They could just drive and drive, nothing but oblivion on either side.

But the causeway didn't last forever, and soon ragged green strips of land reached out toward them like fingers from the mainland. Boats large and small cluttered the shore; rickety docks, some half-demolished, stuck up from the murky low water.

To the left, a few tall buildings crawled out of the misty humidity, and then the city sketched itself in beneath them. It was a low city, but it still made an impression, and everywhere Dan spotted the same kind of Southern idiosyncrasies he had seen since they'd hit Kentucky—old brick architecture sliced up here and there by the odd modern building.

And as their destination, it brought along a breath of relief. Jordan was right, there was only so much fast food and camping a person could take before he started to go a little crazy.

They stopped outside of town for breakfast, convinced by Jordan that the hotdog-in-pastry rollups he called kolaches were suitable for any meal. At least they were fast. Then it was back on the road to head east and into New Orleans proper.

Dan had seen plenty of photographs of the old quarters of the city, but nothing could prepare him for the *feeling* of the place. A streetcar jingled by, tourists clinging to the posts and windows as they ogled the bright, plant-strewn balconies ringed in white filigree ironwork. It was about as close to Europe as one could get in the United States, Dan decided, that feeling from the Pontchartrain Causeway returning—the sense that he was in a foreign world, a place where he maybe didn't belong but wanted to.

Even the streets were odd, cobbled and bumpy. The roads were charmingly crooked, some of the signs as off-kilter as the tourists sloping drunkenly down the sidewalks. It wasn't yet ten in the morning, but that didn't seem to be stopping anyone. Maybe these people still hadn't gone home from the night before. Dan peered down the alleys and streets, hearing snippets of music starting to seep out of storefront niches, songs as good as anything he'd heard on the radio recently.

"Oh my God," Abby said from the backseat. She had rolled down the window, Dan saw, and she was busy snapping photos from the car. "I love it already."

The street music died down as Jordan navigated them through narrow, busted-up streets cluttered with pedestrians who took their time moving to the side. Most of the roads were only wide enough to allow one car and a bicycle through at the same time, and it was slow going, giving Dan plenty of time to take in the archways and stonework, the white plaster statuaries and planters tacked onto almost every pillar and post.

"It's like Disney World," he whispered.

"But with more drunk people," Jordan finished for him.

Uncle Steve lived in the French Quarter, which Dan had always imagined to mean the nice part of town. But his building, which had no parking except for on the street—a situation that made Abby understandably nervous about her car being sideswiped—looked a lot less glossy and tourist friendly than some of the others they had passed on the way in. The red brick, two-story apartment building was right next to a tobacco shop and something called Hernando's Hideaway, which, judging by the chintzy window decor, was almost certainly an adult movie shop.

Jordan carefully parallel parked the Neon, easing into a precariously small spot a few yards down from his uncle's door. *Like Disney World but darker*, Dan thought, climbing out of the car and slinging his backpack over his shoulder. He was caught between two impulses—one to set off in any direction and just see what he could see, the other to dash inside and email Maisie Moore to set up a meeting immediately.

The humidity sucked his breath away, and he wiped at the sweat on his forehead while he waited for Jordan and Abby to join him on the sidewalk. He turned in a slow circle, taking in the opposite building, a squat, black, brick affair with white graffiti marring the side of one entrance. All of the windows and doors looked condemned. This was not Bourbon Street— no parade would turn down here during Mardis Gras. Dan stared at the graffiti, a stark white skull with its mouth open wide. Someone had spray-painted *ne parlent pas mal, les artistes d'os viennent* between the jaws.

Dan took a step off the sidewalk to get a closer look.

"You coming?" Jordan asked.

Turning, Dan found his friends waiting for him on the cement steps leading up to Uncle Steve's door. He'd have to ask Jordan for the translation of the graffiti later. He nodded and lurched forward, catching his foot on the curb, narrowly regaining his balance before he face-planted on the sidewalk.

Jordan chuckled, watching him flail. "He's beauty, he's grace, he's Mr. United States . . ."

"Yeah, yeah," Dan said, flushing. It never felt great to make a fool of himself in front of Abby. "Give me a break. It's been a long trip."

"Too true," Jordan agreed, smacking him amiably on the shoulder and hustling him toward the front door. "But now we're here and I get to settle in." His jaw quivered a little as he stared up at the house. "Dear me," he said. "Welcome home."

Chapter

13

"**H**ey, hey!"

Dan had hardly crossed the threshold into the house before he was swept into a bone-crushing hug. Uncle Steve descended on them like a patchouli-scented giant, tall and broad, with the look of a former athlete gone to good food and cheap alcohol. *This* was Jordan's former Spec-ops uncle? It was hard to swallow. He had bright, glittering eyes and iron-gray hair swept back lazily from a receding hairline. There was a startling resemblance between him and Jordan. They had the same big, round eyes and thin-lipped smile. The same nose, too, although Uncle Steve's looked as if it had been broken and never quite reset.

"The three musketeers arrive," Steve said, looking at his watch. "A few hours earlier than expected, too, but I'm not complaining."

Jordan stood there holding his bags. He didn't seem to know quite what to do. This was his new home, but it probably didn't feel like home yet.

For more reasons than one.

Dan glimpsed a few recycling boxes in the front hall filled to the top with margarita-mixer bottles and beer cans. The only things missing were a surfboard and maybe a bong. "Don't mind the mess. Had a bit of a get-together last night, you know how it goes."

"Totally," Jordan said, nodding slowly. "It's good to see you."

"Right? Too long, man, too long." Uncle Steve pushed back his hair in exactly the same way Dan had seen Jordan do. Then he motioned them deeper into the house. "Well, come on. Shoes off, okay? I'll give you the big tour and then—have you had breakfast? Oh, kolaches? Good man. Okay, then maybe we can help J-man start unpacking."

"Do you mind if I take a shower first?" Abby asked shyly. "It was a long drive."

"Sure! Of course, of course, my bad," Steve said, chuckling and bringing them through to a formal dining room that wasn't, at present, looking so formal. A card table was covered with a wrinkled tablecloth, and dollar-store votive candles were sprinkled about the room. Dan got the feeling Steve didn't spend much time in this part of the apartment.

Still, the floors were wood, and ponderous old chandeliers hung in most of the rooms. In the study adjacent to the kitchen, Steve showed them his jam spot, a cluster of South American drums and flutes collected on a frayed shag rug.

"Some buds come over on Friday nights to jam out," Steve told them, hands on hips. The jam spot was clearly a point of pride. "We won't keep you up too late. Or, hell, you can all join in. Sorry, *heck*."

"It's okay, you can swear. Mom and Dad aren't here to throw a fit," Jordan said, grinning. "Good thing, too, they'd probably try to Pottery Barn the bejesus out of this place."

"Not my style, man, not my style." Steve led them into the kitchen. His worn flip-flops pitter-pattered on the hardwood floors, his loose cotton pants pooling over his feet. "While you're here, help yourself to anything in the fridge. The, uh, grown-up stuff, too, just don't get too wild about it."

He pressed one forefinger to his nose and winked at them. "Any vegetarians in our midst?"

"No, but vegetables kind of sound heavenly after four days of fast food," Abby said, her eyes going a little glossy.

"Right on, right on." Dan couldn't place Steve's accent. East coast, maybe, but slowly descending into a smoother, Creole twang. Steve shuffled over to the refrigerator and bent low to inspect what was inside. "Cauliflower, some bell peppers, and an onion or two. We'll have to do some grocery shopping soon, anyway, so I'll put more vegetables on the list."

Abby thanked him, and then Jordan grabbed a few sodas and made their excuses. They followed Jordan up the narrow staircase to a dark, cool second floor. There were plenty of bags and boxes to unpack from the trunk, but Jordan wanted to relax a little first.

Uncle Steve had hung framed pictures on the wall along the stairwell. Dan paused in front of one of them. It showed three men on a street, or at least outside. The men wore simple masks, with exaggerated eyeholes and long, curved beaks. Dan shuddered, hating the way the black, gaping eyes made the wearers look lifeless, almost as if there was nothing there behind the painted plaster faces. Hopefully there wouldn't be any of those damn pictures in their bedroom or he'd never get to sleep.

"We've got the room at the end of the hall, Dan. Abby's in the office. I know you're probably internet starved so I'll get my laptop set up and grab the Wi-Fi password from Steve." Jordan stopped in the hall and flicked on a light switch, bringing one of

the old chandeliers to life. "You can have first dibs on the bathroom, Abby. Hot water's a little sluggish, so give it a minute."

He led Dan to their room, which was small but reasonably tidy, with two ancient futons in opposite corners, both of them made up with mismatched flannel and cotton sheets.

"This place gives new meaning to the term 'bachelor pad,' but I bet you two will get on famously," Dan said, dropping his backpack onto one of the futons and sitting down. A spring from the frame bounced up to jab him in the rear.

"Hey!" Abby glided in through the open doorway, bringing her camera with her. Her dark eyes slid to where Jordan was booting up his laptop on the table under the window. "Mind if I leave these to upload while I take a shower? I'm running out of space after the cemetery."

"Uh-huh, now it's obvious you two only want me for my computer," Jordan said. He submitted to a playful ruffling of his hair from Abby, then abdicated his chair to her. "All yours. And then yours," he said, glancing at Dan. "You're doing a good job of not saying anything, but I know you're dying to email that Maisie chick."

"Is it that obvious?"

"Yup." Jordan tossed Dan one of the sodas and then cracked his own open. "Jesus, Abby, how many damn pictures did you take?"

"A few?" she answered sheepishly, giving him a goofy smile before zooming out the door. "Thanks!"

"That girl . . ."

Jordan took a few sips from his soda and then placed it on the desk next to his computer. He flung himself back on the

futon, sighing as he nestled down into the pile of blankets and pillows. "Oh, mattress, how I have missed you."

Rather than watch his friend flop back and forth listlessly on the futon, Dan stood and went to the desk, taking a few gulps of the fizzy root beer Jordan had given him. He sat at the folding chair in front of the laptop, watching Abby's files transfer into a new folder, the preview thumbnails popping up every few seconds.

"Wow, yeah, she really did take a lot, didn't she?" Dan moused over a few of the thumbnails. He noticed the pictures from the cemetery, shuddering at the image of the child's jawbone. So she hadn't deleted that photo after all. "Oh, nice. That woman at the library let her take pictures of the gangster's stuff in the archive."

"What was in there? Cigars? A bowler hat?"

Dan leaned closer to the laptop, squinting. The photographs showed an aging cardboard box that was beginning to collapse in on itself, which was placed inside a sturdier wooden box.

"A few postcards, a tin for something, cigarettes maybe . . . an old lighter, a copy of *Julius Caesar*. Weird. Wait, ugh—are those *bones*?"

"What? Awesome!" Jordan popped up from the futon, leaning on the back of Dan's chair to get a look. "Oh, dude, I think those are bones. Fingers maybe? Probably fake."

"Fake? Jordan, he was a gangster. Back in his day, even the medical models of skeletons were real."

Down the hall, he heard the squeak of the shower being turned off.

"Damn," Jordan whispered

"Yeah, damn," Dan said. "I wonder why Abby didn't mention this?"

Chapter 14

*D*an wanted to stay forever in the warm, cozy bubble of feeling brought on by the warm café au lait in his hand and the improbable number of beignets in his stomach. Licking the powdered sugar left on his fingertips, he watched Uncle Steve talk Abby into yet another of the dusty white doughnuts. She didn't put up much of a fight. None of them had.

Cafe Du Monde was nothing like Dan had pictured. For some reason, the name conjured images of writers and poets, silver-haired old men chain-smoking and reading tattered books or scribbling their masterpieces by hand. Instead the café existed in a constant state of bustle, the white and green interior blurred by the constant coming and going of tourists, who stayed for five minutes to get the token experience before trundling away, three or four beignets heavier.

"So what next?" Jordan asked. His loose black tee was dusted with sugar, but in his infinitely cool way it looked intentional, or at least artsy.

Dan felt sticky and slovenly, and glanced around for a place to wash up.

"The market, definitely. It's just there," Steve said, pointing to a wall of the café and what presumably lay beyond. "Anything you want, you can find there. Food, clothes, souvenirs."

They vacated their table, and a server in a paper hat and apron swooped in immediately to tidy it for the next customers. A line stretched out from the back of the café as eager caffeine addicts waited in line for the takeaway window. Jordan and his uncle began to discuss plans for the fall. Jordan was attending Tulane, a private college right here in New Orleans, and Steve was paying, a fact that clearly made Jordan sheepish. His uncle was giving up a lot to help Jordan out with tuition and a place to stay, and Dan couldn't help but admire the man for it.

Dan pulled at his shirt, trying to break the sweaty seal it had formed against his chest. Pennsylvania got hot, but it had nothing like this relentless humidity that sat over the city in a soupy funk. Everyone moved slowly here, as if wading through an actual liquid atmosphere. At least *everyone* was sweaty and gross, which made Dan feel less conspicuous when his hairline dampened.

The sun hung low behind a hazy stream of clouds. Following Steve, Dan let himself be buoyed along by the crowds surging toward the outdoor market. He spotted a long stretch of tents set up in the street, which was wide enough to be a square. Cop cars and wooden blockades kept traffic from turning directly onto the strip where the market buzzed.

The four of them dodged into the shade of the tents, vendors hemming them in on both sides. Counters to buy fresh or cooked seafood sprang up, and stands to buy sandwiches, oysters, lobster. . . . Dan didn't know how it was possible to be hungry again after wolfing down so many pastries, but the smells were intoxicating.

Abby snapped pictures of some of the stranger stands. One selling taxidermied alligator parts interested her in particular.

The shop next door sold a vast array of Mardi Gras masks, from the two-buck plastic junk to handmade masterpieces embellished with beads, crystals, and ostrich plumes.

"Hey, Steve," Dan said, nodding toward the masks. "There's a picture hanging on your stairs of some people in weird masks. And I saw masks like them before, at a library in Shreveport. Is that a thing down here?"

"Oh, those creepy old things." Uncle Steve laughed and smoothed back the gray hair from his forehead. "Back in the day that was the tradition for Mardi Gras. They didn't much use the more ornate Venetian style you see around now. Myself, I found those pictures at a flea market a few years back, thought they fit the house."

That certainly made the masks less creepy, Dan thought, flicking the chin of one of the sparkly, grinning faces that hung from the booth.

Abby lowered her camera, letting it swing by its strap. She shouldered up next to him, her bare, brown arms glistening from the heat.

"What is it with us and masks?" she asked.

"I know. Masks and hoods and motorcycle helmets. Maybe we should buy some of these and see what we're missing," he said. "I saw some of your photos uploading. They look good."

"Thanks." Abby beamed up at him, a tiny spot of powdered sugar stuck to her chin. Dan was about to reach up and wipe it away for her when he felt his phone vibrating in his pocket.

Please be Sandy texting, he silently begged.

He drew out his cell phone. He could already feel his stomach tightening.

Not this again.

Abby read his expression. "It's him, isn't it?"

"Yes," Dan said. "But it's basically blank. Just a few ellipses."

"Can you block the profile? This is getting ridiculous."

Dan agreed, but hadn't this Micah impersonator warned him the other night of the visitors to their tent? He looked up, wondering if maybe this was another warning. Scanning the fringes of the square, he looked for motorcycles, someone photographing them—anything at all suspicious or out of place. But that was just about everything in New Orleans, he decided, seeing two half-dressed women drunkenly grinding against each other outside of a sports bar.

But wait . . .

His eyes focused behind them, and there, sitting on the hood of a red vintage muscle car, were a young man and woman.

It was them—it had to be. Without a second thought, Dan took off running. And this time, he wasn't going to stop until he got some answers.

Chapter

15

"*W*hy are you following us?" Dan shouted as he ran, startling the drunk, dancing girls and a cluster of pigeons out of his way. He hopped the wooden barricade protecting the square from traffic, barreling toward the red car.

"*Why?*" he yelled again.

Already the guy and girl were scrambling to get inside the car. Dan reached the car, sweating hard and out of breath, just as the boy slammed the driver-side door shut. But his window was open and Dan latched on to the edge. A dark-haired guy who looked to be in his twenties stared back, his eyes blazing.

"Who are you?" Dan clung to the window even as the guy turned the key in the ignition. "Why were you photographing me and my friends? What the hell do you want?"

"You want to know who I am? Here." The guy shoved a business card at him. "Meet us later. Eight o'clock sharp. I don't want to talk here, for more reasons than one."

When Dan didn't take his hands off the window, the guy flicked the card at him. It hit him in the neck and then fluttered to the ground, distracting Dan just long enough that the guy had a chance to back down the street into an alley, rolling up his window with a grim look on his face. Still full of adrenaline, Dan stooped to sweep up the card and then took off after the car. Immediately, he collided with a man trying to unpack his trumpet for busking. Dan apologized and tried to keep going, but the car had found a break in the foot traffic, speeding too far ahead for Dan to catch up.

He swore under his breath.

Close. So close.

Dan stared down at the card, finding scrolling black print on an off-white background.

Berkley & Daughters:
Purveyors of the antique, aged, and absurd—since 1898.
New Orleans

No address. No phone number. Just a name and a time. They would have to be enough.

Chapter 16

The sounds of slurping and gulping were almost as loud as the music, and getting more nauseating by the second. Dan stared down at his tray of oysters and then pushed it away, unable to dredge up any enthusiasm for cold, raw shellfish.

Jordan took what Dan refused to eat, spooning red sauce into the craggy shells before bolting it all down.

"I think we should go," Dan said for the third time.

His friends seemed hell-bent on ignoring him.

"What have we learned about this kind of thing?" Jordan asked, lowering his voice so Uncle Steve wouldn't hear. There was little danger of that, though, since Steve was doing just about everything he could to flirt with their waitress. At the moment, he was at the bar "ordering a drink," even though there was table service. "It's usually a trap. Someone winds up hurt or dead. Hardly the way you want to spend your first night in N'Awlins."

Dan sighed, looking down at the Berkley & Daughters card sitting on the red-and-white checked tablecloth. It was barely visible in the low light. He had to wonder why it was so dark in the oyster shack, if not to keep people from actually seeing what they were swallowing.

"Look, whoever is sending messages from Micah's account keeps contacting me whenever these people show up," Dan said, meeting Jordan's eye. "Either they're the ones behind the messages, or there's another connection there, and I want to know what it is. Don't you?"

"Do you think there's going to be a reasonable explanation?" Abby asked, chiming in from across the table. She sipped her sweet tea, then wiped at her chin, only now catching the powdered sugar stain that he'd noticed before. "Do you think it's going to set your mind at ease? Or will it just make things worse?"

Dan stalled, stumped. Put like that . . . "Well, I don't know. But I really don't think this would be that big of a risk. These two didn't seem all that scary up close. Maybe there is a logical explanation."

Wouldn't that be a change of pace?

Jordan chewed at the inside of his cheek, sharing a look with Abby before adjusting his glasses and saying, "Felix didn't seem all that scary at first, either. Neither did any of those students mixed up in the Scarlets. Just because someone *seems* okay up close doesn't mean they're innocent."

"Well, that's a terrible philosophy to take through life," Dan said.

"You're not going to drop this, are you?" Sighing, Jordan finished another oyster and then pushed his empty basket away. "Will you at least let me ask Uncle Steve about this place? It would make me feel better if he knew about it."

That was a bargain Dan could easily make. "By all means."

They waited until Steve returned to the table on his own—to

his credit, he'd actually managed to obtain a new drink—and then Jordan showed him the card.

"Sure, I know it," Uncle Steve said immediately. "Little antique place just a few blocks from the house. They do a mean poetry slam there once a month. Nice family owns it, I think. One of the sons is usually behind the counter."

Dan cleared his throat softly, trying not to look too smug.

"You win," Jordan said, putting up his hands. "Uncle Steve seal of approval granted. Let's just hope this *nice* boy behind the counter is willing to talk."

✗✗✗✗✗

"I feel like the *adults* should have chaperones here," Jordan whispered, pulling Abby and Dan in closer to him as they navigated the New Orleans streets that evening.

"What about us?" Abby asked.

"At least we're sober."

Dan laughed, but it died quickly in his throat. His upper-middle-class suburban neighborhood back home felt totally safe, even quaint, at night. Here, shadows moved between shallow pools of lamplight, and sometimes a laugh or a shout burst out of an open doorway or a window. He could smell the lake, but the humidity dampened the fresh air, and any time they passed by a restaurant, the harsh bite of spices cooking and sizzling overpowered everything else. Groups brushed by them, most too stumbling and rowdy to notice who or what they were knocking into.

"I feel like we're back on a college campus," Abby said. "I'm just glad this isn't too much of a walk from your uncle's."

"So what do you think, Abs? Wanna stay here with me for your big year off?" Jordan asked, grinning. "I bet Steve would let you stay in that office as long as you want."

"It certainly feels . . . artistic . . . here." Her tone didn't ring with interest. "But if I don't stay in New York, I was thinking maybe L.A., just for a real change of pace."

That was about as far from Chicago as it got. Dan wondered if maybe he could convince her to tag along with him, but he decided that was a conversation for another time.

Leaving behind the French Quarter, they passed tattoo parlors open late and a handful of noisy bars, ever more patrons spilling out onto the sidewalk. Then, following the directions on Jordan's phone, they turned onto a quieter side street that ran toward the river, and the noisiness gave way to a calmer nighttime hush. Dan breathed a little easier.

Beyond a bookstore just beginning to close up shop and a candle emporium, they finally found themselves outside a wide storefront window with the name printed across the grimy glass. It was hardly a store that invited you in. Dan could barely make out the BERKLEY & DAUGHTERS in faded gold lettering, and dusty red curtains were drawn behind the panes.

"Charming," Jordan muttered, motioning for Dan to try the door.

It opened with the sound of a tinkling bell. Inside, it was almost pitch-black. A smattering of candles lined the floor, but Dan had to pause with his hand on the door, trying to get his bearings. The red candles, he realized, were giving off an overpowering scent of clove. Gradually his eyes adjusted, and he noticed a small, round table set up just a few yards into the shop.

Four people sat holding hands around the table, a small tray heaped with trinkets centered among them.

"I think it's a séance," Jordan stage-whispered. "Looks like when my friends used to try and freak each other out with Ouija boards in middle school."

Dan tore his eyes away from the strange tableau, drawn by sudden movement in the corner. There was the guy from earlier, watching them from behind a tall wooden counter. He flicked his hand, inviting them over, and Dan inched toward him. This didn't seem like the family establishment Uncle Steve had described, but Dan was determined to settle this.

They shuffled to the counter and then behind it, where Dan discovered a curtain separating the front of the store from a larger and better-lit stock room. He couldn't tell if it was part of the store during the day, but it was filled, floor to ceiling. There were bookshelves in the back and glass cabinets toward the front.

Jewelry; stacks of postcards and photographs; old spectacles; even tiny, delicate animal skulls were all arranged in the glass cases with seemingly no thought given to organization or theme. It was one giant cabinet of curiosities—one Dan admittedly felt tempted to explore.

"You actually showed up," the dark-haired guy said, watching them from where the cabinets transitioned to shelves. "That means Sabrina owes me ten bucks." He came forward and extended a hand to Dan. "Oliver Berkley. Welcome to my humble shop."

"You don't look like a daughter to me," Jordan rasped, leaning against one of the cabinets.

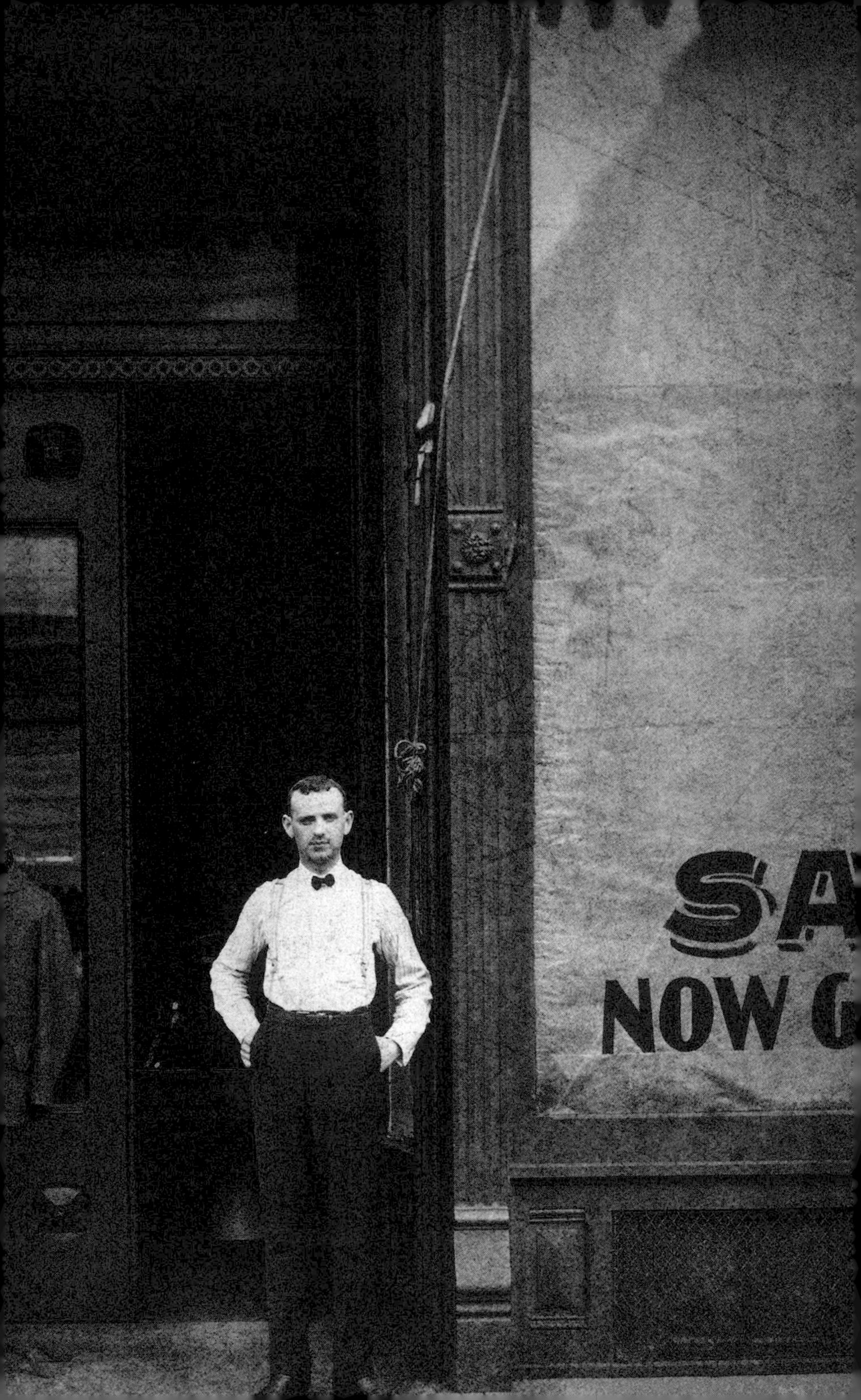
SA
NOW G

Oliver laughed weakly, motioning with one hand for Jordan to get off the cabinet and sticking the other hand into the back pocket of his faded jeans. Tall and thin, he had a classic, almost cherubic look to him, with ruddy cheeks and chestnut brown hair piled carelessly on his head, cropped close at the sides. He'd look like a teenager if it weren't for the small, shiny scar cut diagonally into the curve of his upper lip. Something about that scar gave away his real age. "There were plenty of daughters when the store opened, but that was a few generations ago." His tone dropped its levity. "Now there's only me."

A farther door opened to Oliver's right, and Dan recognized the girl who had been in the car with him earlier.

"This is Sabrina, my girlfriend," Oliver said, introducing a petite black girl with a shaved head and bright, round, hazel eyes. Two tiny silver rings pierced her right nostril.

"They really did show up," she said, smirking and joining Oliver near the shelves. She wore a slashed-up pink tank top over black denim shorts and purple tights. "This kid explain yet how he knew we were following them?"

"I'm not *this kid*," Dan said testily. "My name is Dan Crawford. These are my friends, Jordan and Abby. Really, I think *you* owe *us* an explanation before I say anything else. Why were you following us? And why the hell were you taking pictures?"

Oliver's gray eyes widened in surprise, his thick brows tenting and meeting in the middle. "Whoa, there. Y'all are going ninety in a fifty-five. We didn't take any pictures of you. I was just doing my friend a favor. He said y'all were good with research and the like. Said you could help."

"Help with what?" Abby interjected, pushing farther into the room. She paced, speaking quickly and with her hands, flinging her hair out of her face when it had the audacity to come out of its pins. "What friend are you talking about? I've never seen you people before in my life. How would we have friends in common?"

Dan took her by the arm, squeezing gently. He turned back to Oliver and Sabrina. "She has a point."

"Just let me start from the start," Oliver said, drawing over a metal stool and perching on it. He took a cigarette out of his jeans pocket but didn't light it, instead fiddling with it idly while he spoke, twirling it between his fingers. "Things haven't been great around here the past few years. My old man passed. I got left with the store, and right away, bam, there were break-ins, thefts, graffiti, what have you. I finally thought things had blown over, right, then a few months ago, my dad's grave was tossed. Robbed," he explained, seeing the blank looks on their faces. "My granddaddy's, too. It felt personal, ya know? Like I was being targeted. I finally thought, hey, maybe it was over some rough stuff I got mixed up in a few years back with my buddy Micah—"

Dan froze, and Abby and Jordan both gasped. Oliver and Sabrina stared at him, clearly waiting for him to explain what the big deal was.

"Micah did say he went to juvie for a while," Dan said meekly.

"So you do know him. Good. Thought I was going really damn crazy for a minute there." Oliver blew out a relieved breath, leaning back on the stool. "He said y'all could help, that you dug up some pretty deep dirt back at that school he goes to. Stuff that could help me."

A small, sharp finger wiggled into his ribs. Dan looked over to see Abby staring pleadingly at him, and he nodded.

"Can I, uh, see the messages Micah sent you?" Dan asked, hoping he sounded neutrally curious. "Just to make sure you really do know each other."

"Sure thing," Oliver said, pulling an old iPhone out of his pocket. He maneuvered to the messages and then handed the phone across. "See? 'Dan and his friends Abby and Jordan.' You're all three mentioned right here. We weren't tryin' ta scare you or nothing. It's just, I really have been that desperate for help around here, and Micah . . . Well, I knew he'd be the one who could help me."

Dan scanned the messages. Unlike the ones he had been receiving from "Micah," these all appeared to be made of complete, coherent sentences. And they weren't sporadic warnings, either. There were messages from yesterday, the day before, the day before that. . . . The heat outside didn't matter—Dan felt chilled through.

"Oliver." He felt Jordan and Abby go still and tense beside him as he cleared his throat, handing the phone back and saying softly, "I wish I didn't have to be the one to tell you this, but there's no way Micah really sent those messages. Micah's gone. We saw him die."

Chapter

17

*F*or a long moment nobody moved or spoke. Then Oliver shocked them all by laughing, even snorting a little, before rubbing at his nose. He tucked the cigarette behind his ear and stared down at his phone, still laughing. "That's . . . No, that just ain't right. It ain't possible. It's right here."

Dan shifted. "Those are text messages. Whoever has his phone could send them. You don't . . . you don't have Facebook, do you?"

Which seemed almost as weird as the messages, in a certain light, but Dan let it go. This Ouija-tiny-bird-skull shop didn't exactly scream *normal* or *current*.

"No, I do not," Oliver said slowly.

"If you did," Jordan cut in, "you would have seen Micah's profile get memorialized. That's what happens when . . . you know."

"But how, and I mean—damn. No way. That's—that just can't be true." Oliver's hands shook around the phone until he hid them in his pockets again. "Not Micah. Not him, man. He was a fighter."

"I'm sorry," Dan said. "It's true."

"You said you saw it," Sabrina said, putting an arm around her boyfriend. "How did he die?"

Dan got the impression Sabrina had never met Micah. The way she asked, in such a callous tone and without a hint of emotion, made him think there was no way.

"Not well," Dan mumbled. "I'd really rather not go into details."

Oliver's square chin quivered, but Sabrina's arm anchored him. He slid down against the shelf, but she held him back up.

"Look, you're not crazy," Dan said. *At least not any crazier than I am.* "I've been getting messages from him, too. Mine are really disjointed and don't make very much sense. I think—especially now that I'm seeing yours, too—that someone is playing a nasty prank on us."

"How'd you know him?" Sabrina asked. Oliver didn't look fit to speak just then.

"The three of us met at a summer program at Micah's college," Abby explained gently. "Then we went back for a prospective students' weekend, and that's when we met him. He was Dan's host. I think, well—he was in with a bad crowd, let's leave it at that."

Dan gave her a subtle nod. He didn't think it wise to go into too much detail about the Scarlets. There was no guarantee he could trust these two, even if Oliver really did look broken up at the news.

"He didn't have much family to speak of, even when I knew him," Oliver piped up, swallowing audibly. "Poor kid. And here I was, thinking he was doing better for himself, gettin' somewhere far away from here." He paused, looking at a point next to Jordan's shoulder, his eyes glassy and ready to spill tears.

"You said you and Micah got mixed up in some rough stuff when he was still here," Jordan said. "What did you mean?"

Oliver sighed. "No use keeping it a secret now, I guess. Back before the whole juvie thing, before Micah had to move up to his grandmother's in Shreveport, we used to run jobs for this piece of work who called himself the Artificer. Real covert type—never liked to meet in person. Micah found his ad on craigslist. I ain't know what the hell that was, but Micah knew his way around the computer. Said we could make some real money."

Oliver wiped his nose on his sleeve, and Sabrina took over, rubbing his shoulder as she carried on where he had left off. "What you've got to understand is, things got pretty desperate after Katrina. My family was lucky, all told, but this shop was under six feet of water. Ollie's family was going to go bankrupt."

"I robbed graves for this fucker," Oliver spat out, clenching his jaw. "Micah knew all the lingo in these ads, but I didn't really get it until we got our marching orders. 'Lawn cleanup.' Wasn't no lawn cleanup." He gave a dark laugh. "But, yeah, I was desperate. Micah said it would be no big deal—get the valuables, drop them off somewhere, pick up a check the next week. Trust me, it was one fat check, or I wouldn't have stooped to that level."

"For what it's worth," Dan said, "it didn't seem like Micah was proud of his life down here when I met him, either."

Oliver waved his sympathy away. "Stealing a few necklaces was bad, yeah, but then we were told to take bones. That's . . . that's when I wanted to stop. But Micah, I tell ya, once that boy got an idea in his head, he just didn't quit. He was good at it. He kept saying we were 'trading up.' Fat lot of good all that trading up did him in the end."

He paused and shook his head, resting his palms on his knees and leaning into them. "I couldn't do it. Couldn't take nobody's bones. I took the jewelry, but not the other stuff. The Artificer stiffed me on the check, and I never heard from that guy again—until the graves. That's right. They didn't just take my dad's valuables. They took his bones, Dan. My granddaddy's, too. It's that Artificer, I'm telling you. People like that are evil, and ain't no price high enough for me to mess with what's just plain damn *evil*."

Dan stared at Oliver and Sabrina, stumped on what to say in the face of such a story. It was Abby who finally broke the silence, gesturing back and forth between the boys as if brokering a peace treaty.

"Maybe the messages will stop now, at least," she said. "You said the messages told you to find Dan specifically. Well, maybe this meeting was the whole point. Maybe someone just wanted you to know what happened to your friend, and someone wanted Dan to know the full backstory. To understand what made Micah into the person we knew. You two have met now, and it's all kind of cosmically satisfying, right?"

Now it's all settled, case closed, and we can go back to enjoying our trip, please, her tone seemed to imply.

"You keep sayin' 'someone,'" Oliver said. "But from where I'm standin', it seems pretty clear that the messages are from Micah. He's the one who needed us to find each other, not 'someone.'"

"You've got to be kidding me," Jordan said. Dan didn't respond, even though there was a small part of him that was ready to accept what Oliver was saying. All the pieces fit.

"Okay, don't believe me," Oliver finally said. "But I still don't think we have the full story. Maybe if I got to know you, ya know? Maybe show you around, help you feel welcome in this town."

"We've got my uncle for that," Jordan replied shortly.

"Look," Dan said, "I feel terrible about your shop, and I agree, it's really sick that your family's graves got robbed, but I'm sorry to say, those aren't exactly our problems. Maybe it's best to think of it like Abby said. Micah is at peace now. That's the important thing."

He put out his hand, waiting for Oliver to take it. The taller boy shrugged, but accepted the gesture of goodwill. Goodwill and good-bye.

"I really do hope you can get your . . . *stuff* . . . back," Dan added. "But you already have a cool shop here. Things will turn around. Take my number, okay? In case this Micah thing doesn't, you know, go away."

"Yeah," Sabrina said lightly, dismissing them with a scornful roll of her eyes. "See you around."

Dan took that as their cue to leave. He and his friends huddled back into the front room of the shop, where the dark enveloped them along with the scent of candles and the low chant of the séance group. Dan shivered, and Jordan stepped on his heels, almost pushing him over in his rush to get clear of the shop.

"Roger Berkley, can you hear us? Hear us, Roger, and respond. . . ."

The trio skirted the table and the summoners sitting there. Dan made the mistake of glancing once more in their direction. An older, ginger-haired woman stared back at him. Her eyes were closed, but in the flicker of candlelight, the pale lids of her eyes seemed to glow white, like vacant holes.

Then her eyes snapped open, wide and staring.

"They found me," she whispered fiercely, her eyes rolling back into her head. "Oh. They'll find you, too."

Dan grabbed Jordan's shoulder for balance, then turned and stumbled out of the store.

145

The bell above the door chimed sweetly, and the cloying scent of the candles vanished, obliterated by the humid Louisiana air.

Dan tried to peer back into the store, but he was shut out by the curtains. He moistened his lips, following in the wake of his friends, who had already begun to walk briskly down the sidewalk.

"Holy Creepsville, USA," Jordan whispered, giving an exaggerated shudder. He glanced back at Dan, his lip stud flashing under a sudden flood of lamplight. "Can you believe those weirdos? And that story?"

"Did you hear that?" Dan replied.

"I feel sorry for them." Abby shook her head and waited for Dan to catch up, carefully taking him by the hand. "Not knowing about Micah, and you having to tell them. Dan, I'm so sorry. That must have been awful."

"No, in the store . . ." He stopped, realizing that he was short of breath. His lungs ached. "Did you hear what that woman said to me?"

"No. Dan, I don't think she said anything." Abby let go of his hand, giving Jordan a look that was becoming increasingly familiar and irritating.

"I'm not hearing things," Dan said, not giving a damn if he sounded defensive. "She spoke to me. I saw her eyes open and then she said: 'They found me, they'll find you, too.'"

Jordan flinched. "Jesus. All the more reason to get the hell out of there and never go back." He picked up where Abby left off, going to Dan's side and hooking an arm around his back, coaxing him back toward Uncle Steve's. "Look on the bright side—some chick being creepy at a séance is a big improvement

over being stabbed, set on fire, or chased. For once, we found the people who were following us and they weren't trying to kill us! Hope springs eternal."

Dan nodded, but the pit in his stomach only worsened. He couldn't shake that woman's voice in his head.

They'll find you, too.

He let himself be led back to the house, silent. He didn't have the heart to point out that Jordan was only half-right: they had found Oliver and Sabrina, yes, but neither of them had been the mysterious photographer. Someone else was still out there, following them. And Dan still had a lead to check.

Chapter

18

"**W**hat is it, man? I'm exhausted." And he was. Dan couldn't remember the last time he had felt so bone-tired. Sleeping in a real bed had brought to light all the bumps and discomforts caused by sleeping in a tent so many nights in a row. Now that he had an honest-to-God mattress under his back, he'd let himself succumb to it, sleeping hard, deep, and dreamlessly.

But now Jordan was sitting on the end of Dan's futon, his weight strangely light, hardly making an impression on the duvet.

"What is it?" Dan repeated, groggy.

Jordan sat staring at his hands, then twisted slightly, looking at Dan and grinding his lip piercing against his lower teeth, an anxious gesture Dan had noticed getting worse over the last few days. Jordan didn't say anything; he just watched Dan, unblinking, the little black dot in his lip going around and around.

"Jordan, you—"

He fell abruptly silent, pushing back against his pillow as the piercing in Jordan's lip began to move, then wriggle, then ooze out of his lip, growing into a long, black worm that spilled from Jordan's mouth like a piece of slime. If Dan pulled the covers over his head, this would stop, but his hands refused to obey. Jordan closed his eyes and yawned, his head rolling back as his tongue dissolved into a hundred black worms that dripped down onto the bed. When he opened his eyes again there was nothing there, just two black voids that glittered, trickling down his cheeks in dark rivers, as if his skull was filled with a thick, living oil.

Jordan's pale jaw loosened as if coming unhinged, and that was when Dan regained enough control of his faculties to throw the covers over his head and scream.

The sound woke him out of the nightmare and into another one. Jordan was still there, sitting on the end of his futon. Dan swallowed, shivering as he slid the duvet down and leaned forward, then poked Jordan in the arm.

His friend swayed and woke up, murmuring something incoherent before glancing around and finding Dan there, staring at him wide-eyed and shaky.

"What the hell?" Jordan croaked.

"My thoughts exactly." Dan watched him, suspicious that this too would turn into a hallucination. "Are you . . . Why are you sitting there?"

"Dunno." Jordan squinted down at his hands, then at the empty futon he had vacated. "Must have sleepwalked. Probably in a bed, my body was like: mattress? Comfort? What is this new devilry?" He chuckled to himself, then tilted his head to glance at Dan. "You okay?"

"Yeah. I just had a bad dream. That's all."

"Sorry to wake you up." Jordan stretched and stood, shuffling back over to his futon. Clearly, neither one of them wanted to acknowledge that this had happened before, to both of them. In both cases, the unexplained nighttime vigils belonged to people who had lost it afterwards. It seemed like a bad omen now.

"No more late-night-Houdini antics," Jordan added, crawling into bed. "I promise."

But sleep was now the furthest thing from Dan's mind. He rolled over, waiting until he was reasonably sure Jordan had fallen back to sleep before turning on his phone. Checking the time, he winced. If he couldn't get back to sleep now, he would have a very long day ahead of him.

Oh well.

He crept from the futon to the desk. Nightmare aside, it felt weirdly refreshing to be awake while everyone else in the house was asleep. He really had missed his alone time over the past few days in the car. He never felt fully charged without it.

Dan muted the sound on the laptop, navigating to Jordan's email and the exchange he'd been having with Maisie Moore. Dan reread her last message, then copied her address into his phone. Closing the email and the laptop, he went back to the futon and typed out a message on his phone, asking when she would have time to meet up for lunch. She might think he was weird for sending an email at three in the morning, but at this point, he was way past caring what other people thought was weird.

Before he'd even put his phone to sleep and made a go at falling asleep himself, his phone flashed with a new email.

It was from Maisie Moore.

How about tomorrow at noon? it read. *Or today, I guess it would be. Here are directions to a sub shop I know. Should be easy to find. I was happy to get your message. Haven't been sleeping myself. Not since your friend brought up Evie and Marc. See you soon.*

✗✗✗✗✗

Jordan and Abby tagged along as far as the shop itself, pausing outside while Dan stared up at the sign, bouncing nervously on the balls of his feet.

"Are you sure you don't want us to come with?" Abby asked. She rubbed his arm, but it did little to comfort him.

"It seems kind of personal, Abs," Jordan said. That morning, Dan had gone through the motions of asking Jordan for Maisie's email address and pretending to message her. This was supposed to be the trip when they stopped keeping secrets, but it seemed some habits were hard to kill. "Dan, it's cool if you don't want us to come."

"Thanks, Jordan. And yeah, I think I'd like to talk to her alone. I'll let you know what she says," he answered, leaning toward the door. "I promise."

It was almost noon and the city baked, pockets of hot haze rising up from the sidewalks. Pedestrians took cover under the shop awnings, but there was no escaping the moisture filling the air. Jordan and Abby lingered on the curb for a second, and then Jordan took her by the wrist, tugging her away. "It's broad daylight, Abs, he'll be fine. And anyway, we won't stray far. He can always call if something comes up."

"Exactly," Dan said, giving them a wave. "I won't take long."

He wasn't actually sure about that. If Maisie had known his parents well, then he might want to grill her for hours. Dan dodged into the small, brightly painted shop, going to the expansive deli counter and ordering half a sandwich and a soda. There were only two other people there to eat, a couple cozying up to each other in the corner. Dan took his sub and got a table—the one farthest away from the couple. He forced himself to eat and avoided the temptation of checking his phone every ten seconds. Was she running late or ditching him altogether?

Finally, the bell chimed over the door, and a short, curly-haired woman bustled in. She wore a crisp blue blazer and a matching skirt. A pair of high heels was tucked into her handbag, swapped out for a pair of simple white tennis shoes. She zeroed in on Dan at once, and he blanched, seeing the look of recognition dawn on her face.

"Dan?" she asked, stepping cautiously up to him and offering her hand. "Or is it Daniel?"

"I prefer Dan. It's nice to meet you."

"Yeah. Wow. You—my gosh. There's definitely a resemblance. One second, sweetie, let me grab a coffee." She shook his hand firmly and then hopped over to the counter. A moment later, she rejoined him with a steaming cup of black coffee. "Sorry I'm late. I don't come into the city much."

"It's not that far for you, is it?" he asked, his sandwich forgotten. "Isn't Metairie right next door?"

"It is, but that doesn't matter." She shrugged and hung her bag on the chair next to her. "After the *Whistle* went south, I just couldn't stick around here. I finally settled in at the *Metairie Daily* because they let me work from home. I don't like to leave the house if I can help it, and this place . . . Well, their car crash really did me in. This city just felt all wrong after that."

"Car crash?" Dan's hands curled into trembling fists. "What car crash?"

"Oh, kiddo." Her shoulders drooped. She didn't seem the type to mother anyone much, with her impeccable manicure and flashy handbag, but she reached across the table, patting his wrist lightly. "Your parents. That's how they . . . that's how they went. It was an accident. Just so, so tragic. I thought things were looking up for them and then that. It was awful."

Dan nodded, numb. "I see."

"They were wonderful people, sweetie. It's a damn shame you didn't get to know them." She sighed and sipped her coffee, taking her hand back. "Would you mind showing me those letters you found? I'm not sure I want the memories back, but you went through all this trouble to find me. I might as well take a look."

He couldn't feel his hands as he pulled the letters out of his backpack and pushed them across the table. Abby had insisted on putting them in a ziplock bag to reduce the smell. "They were in an abandoned school in Alabama."

"Arlington," she said, smoothing her palm over the plastic. "It was a dump, but they were desperate. Trax Corp. had more than an army of lawyers out for blood, and the money to put people on their tail. With the warrant for their arrest, there were bounty hunters sniffing around, too."

Dan tried to pull back from the shock of knowing, really knowing, that his parents were gone. Now there was nothing left to do but figure out who they had been and why they hadn't wanted him. Why he hadn't been in the car with them. "I found a police report from a time when my dad got arrested. What was that all about, anyway? What was this Trax Corp. doing?"

"They were a pharmaceutical company. When your parents first started investigating them, it was for rumors of animal cruelty, which was bad enough." Maisie lowered her voice and dipped into her bag, pulling out a stack of papers so thick it took a giant pink rubber band to hold them together. "But that was the tip of the iceberg. They were selling drugs that hadn't passed the safety trials, and of course it was all done under the table, a kind of modern smuggling ring. Your parents found out about it. That's when the real trouble started." She took a long sip of her coffee. "My last year at the *Whistle*, I did one of the most ethically questionable things I've ever done in my life. It's true, your father finally got caught—that must have been the police report you found. I knew he hadn't done anything wrong, but I also knew Trax Corp. had all the ammo. So, I helped put together the money to post your father's bail, reuniting him and Evie, knowing full well they intended to go back on the run. Six months later, investigations into Trax Corp. finally got them shut down, and a week after that, your parents were dead."

She passed him the stack of papers with a sad half smile. "I made copies of everything from that investigation. I know that must seem strange. I honestly didn't know if I was going to give them to you. But you look so much like Marc. Maybe you've got his curiosity, too."

"Unfortunately," Dan mumbled. "And my mom? I couldn't find any trace of her. There's nothing about Evelyn Crawford online, at least not one that seems like she could be my mom."

"Evelyn Ash," Maisie corrected. "Marc and Evie never married. They were a little rebellious like that. Ahead of their time."

"What else?" Dan asked. "What were they like? I mean, before this whole Trax Corp. thing. I just want to *know* them."

"They were smart. Your mother was funny. So, so funny. She hated when I edited her articles; I always took out the snarky bits. But she was a better investigator than she was a writer. She could never keep her opinions out of it, not even close. They'd be proud, I'm sure. You seem like a nice kid."

That's when her phone buzzed, chirping from inside her purse. She jumped, then reached for it, her mouth twitching at the corner. "I . . . should go."

"Are you sure? I feel like I have a million questions." Dan stood with her, watching her snatch up her purse and hurry away from the table. He didn't understand what the sudden rush was.

"Shit. I shouldn't have come here. God, you're an idiot, Maisie." She shoved her phone in her bag, leaving her coffee on the table as she backed toward the door. "Take that stuff," she hissed, nodding toward the stack of papers on the table. "Take it, read it if you have to, but don't tell anyone I gave it to you."

"Ms. Moore, if you'd just—"

The bell rang and the door slammed shut behind her. Dan glanced back at the table, scooping up the papers and shoving them into his backpack before running out after her. The lunch-hour pedestrian traffic swept along the sidewalks, bumping him side to side as he glanced both ways down the street.

He heard a screech of tires and then a scream, followed by a loud, hollow thunk. Dan pushed against the crowd, finding that everyone on the sidewalk had suddenly stopped. He knew it was her. He knew it, and yet he had to see. Why had she run? What had made her panic like that?

Dan broke through to the curb and then stopped, standing perfectly still as gawking pedestrians huddled around him, vying to get a look at the woman lying curled and lifeless under a taxi.

The driver of the cab was nowhere in sight.

Neither was her purse.

Only a fool would think these things were a coincidence.

Chapter 19

"She's *dead*?"

Dan pulled Abby into the closest café and Jordan followed. Coffee cups and bowls of soup had been abandoned at each of the tables. Every shop on the street stood empty. Everyone was still trying to get a look at the gruesome tragedy unfolding on the street. An ambulance siren whined, growing closer and closer.

"She just ran out into the street!" Dan dropped into a booth, pushing aside the teacups left there. "She got a text and then she just up and ran. Something spooked her."

"That poor woman." Abby shook her head, folding her arms on the table and leaning forward, lowering her voice to a whisper. "Who do you think it was?"

"I'd say it was Trax Corp., except we already know they were shut down almost twenty years ago. I don't know. She gave me a giant stack of stuff to look through—maybe there's something in there," he said. He pulled the papers out for them to see, glancing at the barista to make sure they weren't being observed. The workers were too busy clambering over the counter to get a look at the chaos outside.

"Do you have your laptop on you?" Dan asked, pulling the rubber band free from the pages.

"Obviously not. Are you crazy?"

Dan played with the rubber band for a minute, then bound the pages up again. "You're right. We should get out of here. It's going to be even more of a zoo when the police get here."

They slipped through the ring of rubberneckers, the whispers rising around them like a hushed tide. An ambulance had arrived, and EMTs were shoving would-be helpers out of the way to get to the body. They were unfolding a stretcher on the cobbles as Dan turned the corner on the block. It didn't matter how quickly they transferred Maisie to a hospital; he had seen the body, and he was certain there was no saving her.

"I know this goes without saying," Abby whispered as they speed walked back to Steve's apartment building, "but this might be a sign that you shouldn't dig any further into this Trax Corp. thing."

"I'm with Abby. I have to live in this city now, Dan. I don't want it to get weird here."

"It's already weird," Dan muttered. "And anyway, I have these files of hers now. What do you want me to do, throw them away?"

"Maybe!" Jordan shouted, stopping at the foot of the building stairs while Dan sprinted up them. "Just think about it. This was trouble enough to put your parents on the run. They were fugitives, Dan. I know they're your parents, but has it ever occurred to you that maybe they weren't good people?"

Dan skidded to a stop at the door, rounding on his friends staring up at him from the first step. "Yes! It *has*, actually. Considering they abandoned me, the thought had crossed my mind over and over and over again!"

"Well, in case you haven't noticed, Dan, you're not the only one here who's been abandoned by their parents. But you don't see either of us stomping around putting all of our lives in danger. That's all you and your creepy Crawford 'bloodline,' like always."

Dan thundered into the house, not bothering to shut the door behind him. It only stung more that Jordan had made a good point.

"Don't you need my computer?" Jordan called, watching him discard his shoes and clomp across the foyer.

"I'll use Steve's!" Dan shouted, evading them, desperate to be alone.

Chapter

20

*U*ncle Steve's office was empty. It was clear the man didn't spend much time in there, though the ancient computer worked well enough to get him online. Dan slumped down into the office chair, slamming the stack of papers down onto the desk next to him. The fury had gone out of him. Now he just wanted quiet.

As usual, Jordan wasn't wrong. So far Dan had very little to prove that his parents *were* decent people.

Maybe that proof was hidden somewhere in Maisie's collected research. Most of the articles were fairly dry stuff, but Dan ate them up like a man possessed, trying to make organized piles of related stories. There was a lifeline of information in the articles somewhere, he could feel it. But it was finding that lifeline that proved the challenge.

From what he could piece together, it looked like the Trax Corp. investigation, small stakes as Maisie had told him it was over lunch, had uncovered discrepancies the company had successfully hidden up until that point. Dan reopened the articles in order, going back and starting from the beginning.

Trax Corp. Exec Fails to Make the Numbers Add Up
Trax Corp. Hopes to Revive Image with Charity and
Outreach
What Is Trax Corp. Hiding in Troy?

Dan read that last article again. A quick skim wasn't enough. His parents had risked everything over this investigation—enough to drive them to a life on the run from authorities.

For a long moment, he closed his eyes, allowing those thoughts to subside. He plunged back into the article and tried to be as calm and objective as possible. "Sources" had led Maisie Moore to believe that Trax Corp. was smuggling untested, experimental pharmaceuticals to treatment centers and hospitals all over the country. This was worrisome, she concluded, because not only were those drugs not regulated or approved by the FDA, but without proper documentation, there was no telling how long the company had been profiting from the operation off the balance sheets.

Though none of the shipping manifests list the contraband drugs, Trax Corp. has close ties to suppliers like AGI and the Cambridge Group. When reached, neither AGI nor the Cambridge Group agreed to comment for this story.

Dan opened a browser tab and searched for AGI, which turned out to be a now-bankrupt company that acted as a central distribution and logistics center for Kentucky-based hospitals. The Cambridge Group was still in business, he

found, and at last, he thought, reading their company statement, he had found his lifeline.

Proudly serving New England hospitals and facilities since 1962.

He was breathless as he followed the rabbit hole of the Cambridge Group's history. They didn't seem to care about hiding
it—it only took a perfunctory search of their accolades and
awards to find a credible listing of the specific hospitals that
had used them for distribution, buying everything from hospital gowns and bedpans in the old days to supplies like iodine,
penicillin, lithium.

Worcester State Hospital, Danvers State Hospital, Metropolitan State . . .

And Brookline.

Dan stared at the word, feeling for all the world like he had
been slapped hard across the face. Mentally he traced the map
of the hospitals on the list—Missouri, Chicago, then east to
New Hampshire and Brookline. It could be a coincidence, he
allowed, or it could be the one other bond besides blood link-
ing him to his parents.

He started, hearing his phone buzz noisily across the room.
Dan closed down the articles and browser tabs, rubbing his
sleep-deprived and screen-addled eyes.

His relief that the message wasn't from Micah was short-lived.

*Thanks for passing along your number. This is Oliver. Think you can
meet this afternoon? I found something you might want to see.*

Dan sighed, squishing his face down into his cupped hands
and breathing until he could muster the energy to respond.
Maybe it had been a mistake to give Oliver his number. But

he wasn't about to blunder into another creepy séance for no damn reason.

"*What did you find?*" he texted back. "*I'm supposed to be having fun while I'm here, not playing detective.*"

Here's a pic. Any relation?

It took a minute for the photo to load, but once it did, Dan felt his stomach drop out. He knew who they were. Oliver didn't need to send a follow-up message, but he did.

Cleaning. Found in Dad's old desk. Could be wrong, but it looks like you.

He looked younger, happier, than the echo of the man Dan had seen in the Arlington School. But it was definitely the same man, and it was as if Dan was looking at his own face, but more mature, with a tidy dark goatee and a suggestion of dimples under the sharp cheekbones. The woman next to that man was looking over her shoulder, slightly off-camera, her dark red hair bouncing over one shoulder. Well, now he knew where he'd gotten his pointed chin.

"*Why did your dad have that?*" Dan texted back, shaking. "*Why did he have a picture of my parents?*"

Chapter

21

$\mathcal{D}$an managed to slip out the door without alerting Jordan or Abby.

As he crept down the hall and made his way silently down the stairs, he heard soft music coming out from under the door of the guest bedroom. Abby and Jordan were probably in there complaining about him right now. *Well, fine.*

Dan followed the directions on his phone, heading southeast down Decatur toward the heart of the Quarter. He passed row after row of low, two-story buildings with businesses occupying the first floors and housing sitting above. The colors alternated between brown, darker brown, and then peach, brown, brown, peach.

Heavy clouds gathered overhead, making it feel later than it was. The humidity from earlier had only intensified, and the first sprinklings of rain darkened the sidewalks, sending pedestrians huddling under well-used umbrellas.

It was a longer walk than he expected, and Dan couldn't help glancing behind him as he hurried down the blocks; maybe it was lingering fear from being followed and photographed, but he couldn't shake the feeling that he was being watched.

A line out the door greeted him at the hip little coffee joint where Oliver had wanted to meet—something called Spitfire

that had a small, simple sign hanging from the walkway over the greenish-black door. Trying to poke his head inside, Dan nearly ran headlong into Oliver and Sabrina.

"Hey there," Oliver said, handing Dan a to-go cup. "Not many places to sit inside. We can head to the square and find a bench."

Dan didn't argue, openly staring at the folder tucked under the boy's arm. The picture of his parents was inside, and he didn't care if they made him run a marathon through the city, he would get his hands on it.

Coffee was really more Abby's thing, but he sipped the strong brew anyway, noticing that they had dumped a good amount of sugar and cream into his.

"It's not bad," Dan said. "Thanks."

"You didn't strike me as a black coffee kinda dude," Sabrina said, smirking. She looked tired. Come to think of it, so did Oliver. Apparently none of them had slept very well last night.

"So what do you think your dad was doing with a picture of my parents? And why did you only find it now?" Dan asked. He couldn't quite keep the accusatory tone out of his voice.

They walked quickly down St. Peter, the foot traffic growing thicker and thicker until they hit a constant wave of tourists heading toward the famous Jackson Square. The tall, majestic, three-towered silhouette of the Saint Louis Cathedral thrust up toward the rain clouds.

"Cutting right to the chase, I see," Oliver said.

"Can you blame me?"

"Not at all, man. I get it. Shocked me, too. Wasn't sure I was seeing things right, but Sabrina has an eye for faces. She said

there was no way in hell you weren't related to those people somehow." He paused, lowering his head over his coffee cup and breathing in the bitter steam. "Guess this means Micah's not our only common bond."

"That doesn't answer my question. Why did your dad have it?"

"No, I suppose it rightly doesn't, but I also don't have a good answer for you," Oliver said with a shrug. "Not yet. Three heads are better than one, though, right? Or six heads. Where'd your friends get to? Not that I mind. Don't think they like me much."

"We needed a little space," Dan said. "I mean, I'd like to keep them out of this. I have a way of getting people into trouble."

"Oh, lucky us," Sabrina said with a snort.

"It's not like that," Dan hurried to assure her. He drank his coffee a bit too fast, scalding his tongue. Swearing, he followed Oliver and Sabrina to a shaded bench, sitting and squinting into the hubbub of the square. Artists had already set up kiosks and stands, trying to push their wares on wandering tourists.

"I'm not even here for very long," he added. "I just know they want to have a relaxing time before we leave Jordan here. It wouldn't be fair to get them wrapped up in my problems."

"Why *are* you here?" Sabrina asked. Sitting on the end of the bench, she swiveled to watch him over Oliver's shoulder.

"Road trip," he said carefully. He still hadn't revealed that he'd heard them in Shreveport. He was waiting to see if they'd mention it on their own. "We're moving Jordan in with his uncle and having one last hurrah before we go off to college in the fall. Well, before Jordan and I go off to college."

Apparently satisfied with his answer, Sabrina sat back, rubbing one hand thoughtfully over the surface of her shaved head.

"I won't make you wait anymore," Oliver said, setting his coffee down on the bench and opening the folder. He handed Dan the photo, then cupped his coffee with both hands, his knees bouncing as he studied Dan's reaction.

"I didn't know if I'd ever get to see something like this," Dan admitted. He ran his thumb lightly over his mother's face. She was beautiful, pale, and almost fragile looking, but with steel in her eyes. "But I'm glad to have this. Thank you."

"My pop sometimes did favors for certain buyers and friends," Oliver said, resting one ankle on the opposite knee. He scratched at a day or two's worth of stubble. "You run a shop like ours, you get all kinds of folks coming by."

Dan nodded, still gazing down at the photo of his parents. He barely heard what Oliver was saying to him.

"When the old man died a few years ago, I kept most of his stuff just the way it was. Didn't even touch the storage boxes he held for clients and friends. I finally worked up the courage to start looking in them over the past few months, just in case there was something valuable, or something of his," he said. He nodded toward the photograph. "That was in one of the boxes. But there were other things, too. Not sure if they belonged to your folks or not. Nothing was labeled very well. They spend any time in New Orleans?"

Oliver's eyes narrowed, and Dan shifted an inch away from him on the bench. He thought of what Maisie Moore had told him, about the fatal accident that had ruined the city for her. "Yeah. They did. Do you think maybe my parents knew your dad?"

"It's looking that way," Sabrina said. "Still no way of knowing if the junk in that box Ollie found is theirs."

Dan pulled the photo closer to his body, protecting it. "What if I took a look at it? There's still a lot I don't understand about my parents, but maybe something will stand out."

Sabrina snorted into her coffee. For the first time, Dan saw her expression soften. Elbowing Oliver, she said, "Why didn't you just bring that junk?"

"Money's tight these days," Oliver said, flushing and ducking his head. "I wanted to have everything in my dad's storage boxes appraised. I'm sure that sounds greedy."

Dan shrugged. "You don't really know me, I get it. I would like to see it, though, even if you won't let me hold on to any of it. Or I could pay you."

"That doesn't seem right," Oliver replied sullenly. "If I was in your spot, I'd feel entitled to that box. If it was my dad's stuff I'd believe it to be mine, and it'd matter."

Well, that was thoughtful of him. Still, it wasn't like Oliver had brought the box along. If there really were valuables inside, it would be best to get on Oliver's good side and raise the chances of walking away with that box down the line. "Can I ask how your dad died?"

"Car accident," Sabrina said, answering for a visibly uncomfortable Oliver. "Drunk driver ran him off the road and into the river a few years back. We got a real problem with drunk nonsense in this town."

"I'm sorry. It's . . . weird. That's how my parents went, too," Dan murmured. "I thought knowing how they died would make it easier, but it doesn't. Not at all."

"Dan!"

He turned, startled, spilling hot coffee down one side of his pant leg. Abby and Jordan jogged up from around the corner. He recognized that particular shade of scarlet rage on Abby's cheeks.

"Busted," he heard Sabrina whisper.

"Hey." Dan stood, wiped lamely at the stain on his jeans, and, not knowing what else to say, gave a sheepish, "Sorry."

"Any reason in particular you felt like sneaking out on us?" Jordan shot a cool look at Oliver and Sabrina. His glasses were fogged from running in the humidity.

"No need for the side eye." Sabrina stood, placing a hand on Oliver's shoulder. "If we were up to mischief we wouldn't invite your friend here out to a giant public square."

"How did you find me?" Dan put his coffee down on the bench. It was too strong and too caffeinated, and it had soured his stomach.

"You didn't exactly dump all your points into stealth," Jordan muttered.

"What?"

"We followed you," Abby interpreted impatiently. "Steve's house is like a bajillion years old. Everything creaks."

Dan hadn't noticed that, but then, he had been pretty focused on getting his hands on the picture of his parents. A picture that Jordan now noticed him clutching.

"What's that?"

Jordan reached for the picture, and Dan felt a strange, roaring jealousy flare inside. There was a dull hum in his ears, like a distant live wire that buzzed and buzzed. But he let Jordan take the picture, and the feeling subsided. It was just a picture.

"Whoa, damn." Jordan glanced between the picture and Dan, and a second later Abby joined in. "Your dad was a stone-cold fox."

"Thanks?" Dan shifted, uneasy. "Oliver found it in his father's shop, in some storage bins. I think it's possible my parents might have known his." He didn't know if that was information that should be shared, but after their earlier fight, he was feeling the need to show some loyalty to his friends.

Oliver didn't seem to mind. He leaned in to the conversation, rubbing again at his stubble-darkened jaw. "Lots of folks have stored things at the shop. We're still not clear on the connection, but I thought Dan ought to see it."

"Your mom," Abby was saying softly, her brows knit together. "She looks . . . she looks . . ."

"Happy," Dan finished. "I know. It looks like they were pretty close to whoever took this picture."

"Huh. Who says Oliver's dad isn't that whoever? Maybe he was the kind of creeper who gets close to people so he can photograph them without them realizing it. Maybe that runs in the family," Jordan said pointedly.

Dan ignored him. "Can we look at the rest of that box you cleaned out? Like I said, I'm happy to pay you for whatever is inside."

Oliver started to respond, but Sabrina tucked her mouth under his ear, whispering something quickly. He nodded.

"I'll let you have the box. No money required." Oliver leaned back, crossing his arms over his chest. He wasn't necessarily an intimidating guy, but he was tall enough to look down his nose at Dan. "But I want something in return."

"Ugh. The creepers always do," Jordan muttered darkly.

"Dan," Abby warned.

Dan hoped the look he gave Abby was suitably apologetic. He really did feel terrible for dragging them into this—for making the trip all about him, as usual. But he couldn't stop himself. How could he? There was part of him that *needed* to follow this thread, tug on it, unravel it until it all made sense. Why had his dad looked so frightened at Arlington, and why did that make him feel simultaneously sick and hopeful? Like maybe his parents hadn't had a choice in abandoning him? Like maybe there was a crumb somewhere, anywhere, that would finally satisfy his curiosity?

"I want that box," he said again, firmly. "What do you want for it?"

"Your help," Oliver replied. He slipped his phone out of his pocket and navigated to something, then held it out for Dan to take. "These were sent last night. Three solid hours of messages. Not like the old ones. They're like yours now. I don't know what this means, but damn it, he was my friend. I need to find out."

Dan took the phone, his spine tightening until his shoulders recoiled. He could feel Jordan and Abby breathing on either side of his neck, craning to see the message, the single line repeated hundreds of times over.

Micah might have let Dan rest for one night, but Oliver wasn't nearly so lucky.

the y ha ve m y bon es
th ey hav emy b o nes
they have my bones

177

Chapter
22

"*A*nd just what are we supposed to do with that thrilling bit of information?" Jordan demanded, tearing his eyes away from the phone and the messages. "Who is he talking about, 'they'?"

"I told you," Oliver said, tugging the phone out of Dan's grasp. "The people Micah and I got mixed up with were evil. When you're involved with them, it's for life. And beyond, it looks like." He sat back down, puzzling over his own words while chewing his lower lip.

"And do you think these messages are really coming from Micah's ghost or spirit or whatever?"

Oliver nodded.

Jordan had started to pace. Now he grabbed Dan's unfinished coffee and started to drink it. "We saw Micah die. In New Hampshire. Whatever shenanigans you two got up to here in high school have nothing to do with it."

"Maybe not," Abby reasoned, "but remains are usually returned to a family for burial. If Micah didn't have any family up there to take them, then maybe they ended up back in Shreveport. Or . . . or, well, in a place that he doesn't like. As a dead person. God, I can't believe I just said that aloud."

That drew a chuckle from Sabrina. "I'm inclined to think it's

BS, too," she said, cocking her hip to one side. "But I can't deny sixty-three messages from a dead kid on Ollie's phone."

"Is there any way to get in touch with your former employer? The Artificer, you called him? I know that was years ago." Dan joined Oliver on the bench, resting his elbows on his knees. He had taken the photo of his parents back from Jordan, and he smoothed it carefully.

Oliver thought about this for a moment. "I've tried calling the number we used," he said. "It's been disconnected for a long time. If there was anything online or another number, I don't know about it. Micah was the one who set it all up."

"There was a drop spot, though," Sabrina said. Her bright, hazel-green eyes widened, catching the sun as she added excitedly, "A mailbox, yeah? You told me you two would use some mailbox in the middle of damn nowhere to communicate."

"Not really 'communicate.' We did get our assignments there when we were first starting out, and they'd always come with instructions for where to leave what we found. I suppose it's something," Oliver said. He didn't mimic her enthusiasm. "Long shot, if you ask me."

"Better than nothing." Dan shrugged and stood, watching Jordan chug the last of his coffee. "So how do we do this? Where's the mailbox?"

"It's on Roman, but it's a drive. We'll have to take my car."

"That's fine. Let's go," Dan replied.

"Can't, not now—gotta get back to the shop before I lose a full day of business. But we can head over after closing. If things are slow I'll shut the place down early."

"Of freaking course it has to be at night." Jordan rolled his

eyes. "Why don't you just give us the address and we can go now? You know, streamline the process a little."

Sabrina burst out laughing, shaking her head. "Yeah. No. You three should not be going anywhere near the Ninth Ward alone. You're tourists. Just trust me, it would not go well for you."

"And you're gonna be, what, our bodyguards?" Jordan shot back defensively.

"Look, the French Quarter it is not. It's better if Ollie's there. One quick look and then we can go."

For a second, Dan was certain Jordan was going to press the idea of going without their help. Dan didn't relish the idea of exploring a grave robber's old stomping grounds without a get-away car in close proximity, and somehow he didn't think Uncle Steve would be game to chaperone.

"You're here on vacation, to have fun," Oliver said gently, pleadingly. "So have fun. Put all this out of your head for a few hours and enjoy the city. We'll catch up with you tonight."

✗✗✗✗✗

They managed to take Oliver's advice, for the most part, at least. Abby and Jordan seemed more than happy to forget all about Oliver and Micah and hit the outdoor market again to shop for souvenirs. A short trip back to Uncle Steve's had allowed Abby to grab her camera, and she didn't hesitate to drag them all over the historic areas she wanted to capture.

Dan remained a million miles away. Or maybe just eighteen years away, back to when his parents had uncovered the corruption at Trax Corp. and died because of it. Was it really worth Dan risking all their lives in the same way to find out what was happening here now? He knew he should at least tell Jordan and Abby about the connection he'd found from Trax Corp. to Brookline, so they'd know how deep it all ran. But like the picture of his parents, he was jealous of the information, holding it close as if it was a prized possession.

Plus, even with Abby photographing and Jordan giving a nonsensical, made-up guided tour of everywhere they went, Dan already sensed their unease. Not with each other, but with him. No one brought up what had happened with Maisie Moore that afternoon or the picture of his parents. It was like they were determined to pretend none of it was happening.

Just before dinnertime, they returned to Uncle Steve's. The door to the building was open, and a man and a young woman stood on the stoop, chatting with Steve. Jordan's uncle leaned against the door to prop it open, a half-smoked cigarette tucked behind one ear.

Dan, Jordan, and Abby paused at the bottom of the stairs, sharing a glance while obviously eavesdropping.

"Friends of your uncle's?" Dan asked.

"Never seen 'em before in my life, but now doesn't seem like the time to make new friends," Jordan replied. He had bought a monumental number of board games at a bookshop they'd found, and now he was sinking under the weight of the shopping bags.

"They look fancy," Abby added in a whisper. Her dark eyes drifted to the young woman. "I *need* her dress."

"Well, you know I absolutely depend on your vote this year,"

the man was saying. He was tall and, as Abby had noted, well dressed. Dan didn't know the first thing about designer clothes, but even he could tell the man's suit was probably worth a small fortune. The two made a tidy pair, him in light, summery gray and her in a peach-colored sleeveless dress.

Jordan took one step up toward the door and the others followed.

"What happens in the voting booth stays in the voting booth," Uncle Steve replied, but he winked.

The other man laughed, jutting out his hand and taking Steve's, pumping it vigorously. Dan didn't tend to like politicians, but the man had an infectious energy to him and a laugh that was warm and booming.

"You're a pillar of the community, Mr. Lipcott, and having your vote is a true honor."

"*Pillar of the community?*" Jordan repeated in an undertone. He snorted, setting his heavy bags down on the cement stairs. "What a load of—"

"Ah! And who are these three bright young things? Are they of voting age?" The man opened his hands wide as if to hug all three of them in one go. The woman turned, too. Dan had a hard time not staring; she was stunningly pretty, with glossy dark skin and hazel eyes like Abby's. Her lips were lacquered red. It looked like someone had cut her hair with a very sharp razor.

She hugged a clipboard to her chest, eyeing them up and down with a pinched smile.

Dan looked away. Her eyes made him want to wither on the spot.

"This is my nephew, Jordan," Uncle Steve said, shuffling out

another few steps onto the stoop. "His friends are just visiting for a summer vacay and helping him settle in. He's moving here for a bit. They've been scampering all over the city, making friends with the folks over at Berkley and Daughters. Kids, this is Connor Finnoway—sorry—*Councilman* Connor Finnoway. He's running for reelection and shamelessly courting my vote. But he plays a mean saxophone, so I don't mind too much."

The councilman gave another booming crack of a laugh and turned to smack Uncle Steve on the arm good-naturedly. "Shameless, yes, and not too proud to admit it." His green eyes sparkled behind a big, patrician nose. His hair was thinning and almost bald on top, but it didn't detract from the bright, youthful energy that poured out of him.

Some people were just born to be politicians.

"You made a fine choice by visiting our city. I trust you're enjoying yourselves so far? Oh, and you have a photographer among you, too." He adjusted his tie and took a step down toward them, gesturing to the camera around Abby's neck. Dan suddenly didn't like the man's enthusiasm or his smooth smile.

"Yeah, I'm doing a photo project about some of the old gin runners that used to operate in the South. It's a fascinating history," she said.

"Any history buff worth their salt visits Madame A's while they're in town. Berkley's is nice, but it can't hold a candle to her establishment," Mr. Finnoway said, glancing first to his assistant and then to Steve for confirmation. He was given enthusiastic nods. Then his eyes redirected to Dan and lingered. "It's really not far. Here, I'll show you."

His assistant offered him his phone. He deftly brought up a

street view of the neighborhood and traced his finger along the route for her.

"See? A brief walk from here. It's an absolute treasure trove for the hungry historian," he said, chuckling. "I go often myself."

"You're a historian?" Abby asked, her brow furrowing as she studied the map.

"Oh! No," he laughed, throwing back his head. "Dentist by trade, but it can get a bit grim staring down throats all day. We all need our hobbies, right? And one would have to be dead inside not to love history, living in a place like this."

"It's a shame you can't be there to show them around the shop yourself," Steve said, smiling. "That place can be overwhelming for first timers."

Mr. Finnoway actually paused to consider this.

"Say, Tamsin, what's my schedule like tomorrow afternoon?"

"Busy, sir. But Ms. Canterbury did cancel her noon appointment."

"Fantastic." The councilman clapped his huge hands together and then opened them again. "Why don't I join you all over my lunch break and show you the lay of the land?"

"Take it easy now, Connor, they don't live in the state. Hardly future constituents for you to butter up," Uncle Steve said with a snort. It was the exact snort Jordan gave so often.

But Abby was already nodding and hugging her camera. "Would you? That would be amazing."

"Tomorrow around noon then," Finnoway said. He glided past them down the stairs, his assistant following. A sharp, lingering perfume followed her. Dan didn't know how anything could smell *French*, but she did.

"Get out of here, you old rascal," Uncle Steve called, waving to the backs of Finnoway and the woman. With one last burst of strength, Jordan gathered up all his bags and pushed up the rest of the stairs. "Did you buy the whole store?" Steve asked, grabbing one of the bags to help.

"Making decisions is too depressing. . . ." The rest of their conversation was lost as Dan and Abby trailed behind.

"It'll be fun to see that shop tomorrow," she said. "I know your mind is on other things, but we should try to relax a little, too."

Dan nodded, but relaxing was out of the picture. "Let's get something to eat. Oliver will be calling soon."

Chapter

23

*D*an pressed his nose to the window, staring out into the bleak, naked expanses of the northern neighborhood. It was immediately and terribly apparent why Sabrina had refused to let them go alone; the houses on these blocks were sparse, entire lots emptied and never reclaimed after the hurricane had washed them away.

The devastation rippled visibly across the neighborhood. The farther they went, the worse it got. It was destruction on a level Dan had never seen before, and scariest of all was the fact that they were just a few miles from the vibrant French Quarter. He watched the road wander in and out, no real edge to it, its surface so pocked with holes they could barely go above fifteen miles an hour.

The sad silence that had descended over the car was interrupted by the sound of Dan's phone dinging. For obvious reasons, they all tensed—but it was only Sandy texting. She wanted to know how his second full day in New Orleans had gone. The empty message return box glowed up at him, so tiny and inadequate to answer that question.

We're having tons of fun, sorry for not messaging sooner. What kind of souvenirs do you guys want?

He returned to staring out the window, turning from one unhappy thought to another.

"There's people with heart here," Sabrina said to no one in particular from the passenger seat, slicing through the silence. "And they don't want your pity."

"It's not pity," Dan said. He didn't know *what* it was. "I just . . . didn't expect it to look like this."

Abby had brought her camera but hadn't lifted it once since they'd entered the fringes of the dilapidated streets.

"You weren't dumb enough to tell your family where you were going, were you?" she asked.

"No," Jordan answered. "Uncle Steve wanted to take us on a barge ride. I told him you guys were taking us to a concert."

They were quiet for the length of a few more blocks, and then Oliver slowed the old Challenger and veered to the side of the road. A light came on in the house two lots down, and Dan stiffened. A dog barked in a long, lonesome wail. The streets weren't exactly empty, and each driver who moved to pass them gave their car a thorough look.

"Let's make this quick," Oliver muttered, kicking open his door.

He told Sabrina to wait in the car and left it running. Abby and Jordan chose to wait in the car, too, but that was fine. The fewer of them out in the open, the less attention it would draw. It was hard to see, but Oliver and Dan used their phones to give themselves minimal visibility.

"This area is seriously rough," Oliver said. "I don't know if that's why the Artificer chose it, but there it is." He moved swiftly to a mailbox sitting at the edge of a bedraggled lawn. A few sluggish weeds poked up from what had been a sidewalk.

The mailbox was crooked, slumped over, the box perching at such a severe angle it seemed to be regarding them skeptically.

Someone dumped a bag of garbage into a bin a block or so away, the sound of shattering bottles sending a finger of cold up Dan's spine.

"Hold this," Oliver said, shoving his phone into Dan's hands. He worked by the tiny bit of light, yanking on the lid of the mailbox until it gave with a screech of protest. It looked to Dan like there was nothing inside, but all the same, Oliver thrust his hand into the open box and groped around the edges. "Christ, I'm gonna need a tetanus shot after this."

He withdrew his hand, and a tattered, waterlogged scrap of cardboard was pinched between two fingers.

"Is that it? A new assignment?" Dan asked.

"That's it. Now we're getting out of here."

They swapped, Dan taking what Oliver had found and the other boy taking back his phone. That noisy dog bayed again, closer, and Dan half threw himself into the backseat. Oliver pulled away from the curb, making a messy U-turn and then picking up speed.

"Find anything?" Abby asked.

"Yeah," Dan replied, holding up the piece of cardboard for her to see. Using his phone for light, he leaned back in the seat and examined what they had unearthed. "Looks like a post-card maybe."

He held the light to the cardboard and then brought it close to his face. There was faded writing on it, and the pen had cut so deeply into the paper that he could see the indented slices behind the ink.

"Hang on," he said, reading. "I don't think this is an assignment. It's a poem, and I've seen it before."

"What? How?" Sabrina blurted.

"Listen." He held up his hand, taking a deep, shuddering breath before reading over the familiar lines. It was longer than he remembered. This time, it sounded complete. "'Be not too happy nor too proud, beware your luck, crow not too loud; the Bone Artist steals and then he leaves: the Bone Artist, the Conjurer, the Prince of the Body Thieves.'"

Chapter 24

The car rolled along steadily, bumping now and then, but that rhythmic jostling only made him drowsier. Dan struggled to keep his eyes open. He felt drugged, like he had been awake for days on end, sheer willpower alone keeping him upright. It was a sudden feeling and all encompassing; even his *toes* felt tired.

It didn't seem natural, which made him think it would pass. He was starting to feel anxious about it, and he put his hand in his pocket to grab his meds before realizing he'd left them at Uncle Steve's. He leaned to look past the center console at the windshield. They started to speed up, accelerating so abruptly he felt his stomach give a nauseating jerk. He tried to focus his eyes, watching the road twist and then straighten—and then drop out altogether. There was nothing in front of them, just empty space and what looked like a distant line of trees.

Dan called out. He didn't know what he ended up saying, but he wanted it to be, "We're going over the edge!"

Driver and passenger spun around to look at him. It wasn't Oliver and Sabrina. Shouldn't it have been Oliver and Sabrina? Dan flattened himself back against the seat, shaking.

They had no faces. God, there was nothing there at all. They were just blanks with bodies and hair, heads like clean, white ovals, like eggs turned on their points. The faceless faces hovered in front of the bleak oncoming landscape as the car veered off the cliff edge, and then they were suspended. They watched Dan silently. How could they watch him without eyes? But he felt it, the full weight of their attention pinned on him.

For a second he was weightless inside the fear, rising up as the car plummeted down toward a blur of blue and white foam. A river. They would hit it any second now. He closed his eyes and braced, waiting for the final, hard crunch of impact.

Instead he flew awake in his bed, gasping so loudly and desperately his throat felt instantly raw.

For a full minute he couldn't remember what had come before—there'd been the car ride, and finding the postcard with the poem, and then . . . ? When he thought about it, hard, the memories started to come back, as if they were from a year ago and not from last night. Oliver had had no idea what the poem was supposed to be—it didn't look like the assignments he used to get—but Jordan had remembered the poem, too, from the library in Shreveport. They had all agreed to regroup at Oliver's shop tonight after it closed.

Dan grabbed the top sheet and wiped his sweaty face across it. He didn't want to close his eyes again, terrified of the white faces.

The room was already bright with morning sun, and though he didn't feel rested, a quick glance at his phone confirmed he had slept through the night. Any minute now, Abby would be knocking on the door to make sure they were awake.

Dan got up and put on a faded T-shirt. When the knock came, Dan was surprised to find that not only had Abby showered and gotten dressed, she'd come armed with three coffees and a bag of beignets.

"You went out?" Dan croaked, opening the door fully for her. She breezed in, setting the drinks down on the table with Jordan's computer.

Jordan groaned and huddled under the sheets, pretend sobbing when she yanked the blinds open.

"Yeah, I couldn't sleep in."

"I can always sleep in," Jordan whimpered, still hiding.

"And anyway Steve was up, too, so we did our morning yoga together and then went out to get breakfast for everyone."

"Of course you did." Dan smiled wanly at her, wishing he had a fraction of her taste for mornings.

"So I've been thinking," she said, turning and flouncing down onto the chair in front of Jordan's laptop, "what if this poem is like some kind of anthem for the people Micah worked for? Think about it, they definitely deal in bones, right? The 'bone artists'? It makes sense."

"Would you slow down? My brain's still booting up," Jordan murmured, finally crawling out of his cocoon of blankets. It was the first time Dan had seen his hair look truly unkempt instead of stylishly messy.

Abby zoomed onward, gesturing with half a beignet in her hand.

"I think we should ask that councilman about it today," she added.

"No." The response was automatic. Jordan and Abby both paused and stared at him. Dan shrugged. "I just think he's too friendly, you know? Nobody should be that friendly."

"That's the most depressing thing you've ever said," Jordan said, rolling onto his back. He punched a few pillows into shape and wedged them under his head. "Although Uncle Steve does say you should never trust anybody in a suit that costs more than a car."

"Uncle Steve is an aging hippie," Abby countered.

It was a little vicious. Jordan sputtered.

"What? It doesn't make him any less lovable, but it's true."

"I just think it's better if we keep all of this between us," Dan said, redirecting. "This bone stuff is creepy."

"Us and Oliver and Sabrina, you mean."

"Abby . . . Okay, yes, between the five of us, then."

Jordan held out an empty hand, opening and closing his fist until a beignet landed in it, thanks to Abby. "Let's rewind for a minute here. What do we actually *know* from the poem? What did it show up on before?"

"On the newsprint you and Dan *borrowed* from the archives in Shreveport," Abby said impatiently. "Not that I'm complaining, I guess. I know you grabbed that article for me."

"An article about that gangster you're researching," Dan added, regarding her evenly over his coffee. "Which is, I'm guessing, the reason you're so interested in the whole situation today."

She took the accusation in stride, wiping the powdered sugar from her hands. "Fair enough, yes, there appears to be some overlap between Oliver's former employers and Jimmy Orsini. Can you blame me for wanting to know more? This is a project I've been thinking about all summer, so *pardon me* if I'd like to follow up on this connection."

"I'm *glad*, Abby. It's nice not to feel like the Lone Ranger in this," Dan replied. "And I think you're right. We shouldn't overlook anything as coincidence at this point."

"Then we agree," Abby said, lifting her chin into the air. "We'll ask the councilman about it today."

"I didn't say that—"

"God, it's too early to argue," Jordan interrupted, shutting both of them up. "We'll flip a coin before we head to the store. There? See? Now someone hand me a coffee before I get grumpy for real."

Chapter 25

*M*adame A's, a sloped, mauve-colored storefront, was not on any street Dan could discern; it huddled between the sidewalk and a back alley, a single dingy lantern and sign whispering its presence.

A strong reek of hot garbage wafted toward them from the shadowy courtyard at the end of the alley. The familiar, discordant whine of jazz musicians warming up—fiddle and trumpet and saxophone clashing against one another—drifted just above the stench, which was so thick it seemed to have its own bitter flavor.

"What an interesting smell we've discovered," Jordan mumbled dryly, sticking close to his friends, wedged right in the middle of them.

The windows of the shop were blacked out, smudged with paint or grease. A cat wandered out to meet them, a one-eyed calico with three quarters of a tail. It watched them with its little fuzzy chin tilted up and imperiously to the side. The door to Madame A's was already open a fraction, a curtain behind the door perfectly still in the rank doldrums of the alleyway.

"After you," Dan said, gesturing for Abby to go first. "This being your idea and all."

"Let's just hope it smells better on the inside," she whispered, taking a hesitant gulp of air before plunging through the curtain.

The atmosphere inside the antique shop wasn't exactly pleasant, but it was at least well lit, and the garbage smell was replaced by the overpowering perfume of jasmine incense. The place did remind Dan a little of the back room in Oliver's shop, but it was even more crowded here and far less organized. The ceiling was cluttered with mobiles, some made from beads and crystals, others of bone and feather. The far wall was covered with a giant display of candles, bottles, flags, and tiny tincture pots. A crooked sign had been posted above it, reading: *CANDLES— OILS—DRAPO—CONJURE HAND RUBS.*

Dan wandered over to inspect the display, dodging propped-up glass cases filled with pamphlets, books, and jewelry. After all the talk about grave robbing, Dan couldn't look at valuables like this without imagining who had once owned them, and when they'd been lost. Then, another gust of jasmine-scented air rolled through the shop. A haze of smoke made the room feel small and dreamlike.

Dan picked up one of the candles, inspecting the label.

"'*Les Morts*,'" he read softly.

"It's for Voudon practitioners."

Dan set down the candle with a quick swivel of his head. He was no longer alone at the display, but he hadn't heard Connor Finnoway approach. The councilman, taller than Dan by a head, reached over his shoulder and took the same candle, turning it slowly in his hand.

"It's a misunderstood religion," the councilman added with a smile. "Most of these candles are for luck, for health, for love. Nothing sinister about it."

Dan nodded, but he wasn't so sure. His French wasn't great, but he didn't know how anything called *Les Morts* could be for luck, health, or love.

The councilman had changed suits, though this one was just as slick as the last. The watch on his left wrist sparkled with diamonds.

"Mr. Finnoway?" Abby joined them. "Thanks for meeting us. I had some questions for you."

"Ah. No preamble," he said, chuckling. He turned to Dan but pointed at Abby. "Very concise. I like that."

Dan didn't care what he liked. He wasn't crazy about the idea of asking Finnoway about the poem they had found, but Abby had won the coin toss. Across the room, Jordan was busy talking to a tall, willowy woman with glittering dark eyes and skin. It was impossible to tell how old she was; her features appeared delicate, timeless. The way she seemed to rule over the shop without lifting a finger or saying a word made Dan think she must be the eponymous Madame A.

"There's this verse," Abby was already saying, offering the councilman a version of the poem she had copied down onto a fresh sheet of paper. "We've seen it twice now—once in Shreveport and once here in New Orleans. We were wondering if it means anything to locals."

Finnoway browsed the paper, one eyebrow quirking up in interest. "And what did Steve Lipcott have to say about it?"

Abby blushed, glancing side to side. "I didn't actually ask him. He didn't grow up here."

"Smart of you to consult a native." The councilman grinned, then handed the poem back to Abby. "I've heard it before, but not since childhood. It's a sort of nursery school rhyme, our version of a boogeyman. You know, eat your broccoli, say your prayers, or the Bone Artists will come and take off your toes."

Dan glanced at Abby, but she apparently had the same thought, and she vocalized it first. "That seems awfully harsh. I mean, do you really tell children someone will take their bones?"

"Hansel and Gretel are fattened up to be eaten. Stories for children have always leaned toward the macabre." He grinned, showing perfectly even and white teeth. "At any rate, it's not a popular story here anymore." He nodded toward the poem in her hand. "That's about as vintage as anything you'd find in this store."

"So they're not real then?" Dan asked coolly. "These Bone Artists?"

Finnoway laughed and turned back to look at the candles. "I didn't say that, did I?"

Abby rolled her eyes and reshuffled her papers. "Now you're just teasing us."

"A cautionary tale doesn't work, my dear, if nobody believes it."

The curtain over the shop's door rustled, and Dan twisted to look, finding that Finnoway's assistant had come in, too. She appeared to be looking for the councilman.

Dan didn't mean to stare, but she was mesmerizing, so precisely coiffed and dressed she looked ready to stroll onto a movie set. He heard Abby cough lightly, then cough a little louder.

Idiot. Abby was *right there*.

"Excuse me for one moment," Finnoway said, going to confer with his assistant by the entrance.

After an awkward moment of silence, Abby said, "This trip hasn't been even close to what we were expecting, has it? But things are okay, right? Are you doing okay?"

"Sure, let's go with okay," he said. He raked both hands through his messy hair and dodged around the case of necklaces to the wall. There was a globbed line of paint running horizontally across the plaster. "Honestly, I don't know what I'm feeling, Abby. Sad? Confused? Angry?"

He traced the thick, painted line with his fingertips, reading the numbers penned above it. It was just a date, and Dan shivered, realizing the line was marking how high the water had risen in here during the hurricane. It was a miracle anything in the store had survived.

"Angry?" Abby paused, her fingers hovering over a rotating display of postcards and laminated newspapers. "Angry at who? Your parents?"

"A little bit, yeah. And at Oliver, too. He should have just given me that damn box. It's not like he needs the stupid thing, and it might actually tell me something about why my parents gave me up. Maybe I'm looking too hard for something that isn't there. Maybe they thought they were doing something good. But I just can't figure out why I was shuffled around Pennsylvania while they were killed in a car crash in Louisiana." He sighed and leaned against the wall. "The point is, I don't think I should have to bargain for something that should be mine."

He trailed off, watching Finnoway wander back to them.

"I was hoping to borrow you for a moment," Finnoway said, but while Dan expected that to be directed at Abby, it wasn't.

"Oh. Wait, me?"

"Yes." The councilman nodded toward a quieter corner away from the counter and his friends. "I didn't get a chance to say this yesterday, but when Steve mentioned you were hanging around with the owner of Berkley and Daughters, well . . ."

"Oliver?" Dan narrowed his eyes, wondering why exactly they needed to be speaking in hushed tones. "What about him?"

"He's not exactly the most savory fellow. His father had a reputation for being a notorious drunk. And in this city, that's saying something." Clearing his throat, the councilman glanced over his shoulder at Abby, watching her for an uncomfortably long moment. "I'm not here to help your girlfriend pick out souvenirs, young man. I'm here to give you a bit of advice."

"Why do you care what I do?"

"I don't." He put his hands in his pockets, twisting away from the shelves of knickknacks. The politician's smile from yesterday was gone, replaced with an angry grimace. "Oliver Berkley is a pimple on the ass of this city, just like his father and his father's father. Steve Lipcott is an old friend, and if his nephew is going to be living here, I wouldn't want his reputation or Steve's to be tainted by . . . unfortunate associations."

Dan ground his teeth together, staring up into the councilman's inscrutable green eyes. "Is that all?"

"That's all."

Smiling, Finnoway glided away from the shelves, smoothly cutting into Abby's conversation with Madame A. Dan abandoned his spot at the wall, joining Jordan instead. Apparently Madame A had talked Jordan into buying a large handful of candles; they peeked out of Jordan's bag as his friend swung around to greet him.

"They're for Steve," he said immediately. "I thought I'd pick him up something while we were here."

"Uh-huh." Dan peered at Madame A behind her counter. She looked persuasive enough to get a person to buy just about anything.

"Any luck with the friendly councilman?" Jordan asked. A complimentary tea tray had been set out on a countertop near the door and Jordan was headed there, beelining for the sugar-dusted cakes arranged on a silver plate.

"Not really. Before he had some not-so-nice things to say about Oliver, he said the poem was just some dumb fairy tale used to spook children into behaving."

Jordan's brows shot up as he shoved a teacake into his mouth. "Really? No way, that's not what Madame A said."

"Oh? And what did Madame A have to say about it?" Dan lowered his voice, shooting a glance over his shoulder to make sure Finnoway and his assistant weren't listening in. The assistant was on a phone call, hissing into the mobile and pacing.

"She said the Bone Artist thing started out as a legend, yeah, but that there was a kernel of truth to it." Jordan matched Dan's conspiratorial whisper. He leaned in, pouring himself a cup of pale, greenish tea. "Back during the Depression, people were so desperate for money that they started grave robbing. Apparently, around here, there was a group of people called the Bone Artists who would pay money for *bones*. The bones supposedly contained some of the dead person's personality, and the Bone Artists claimed they could turn the bones into talismans to sell back for even more. So if you wanted luck, you found a lucky person's bone and turned it over, or if you wanted money you took a rich person's." Jordan blew the rising steam away from his cup of tea and dunked a second cake into it. "It was big business. I guess people get real superstitious when shit hits the fan."

Dan shivered. "Jesus."

"Yeah. Sounds a bit like Oliver's Artificer guy, doesn't it?"

It did. Dan checked on the councilman again, who was chuckling in his supremely infuriating way with Abby over some article they had found. "Why would Finnoway lie about it?"

"Who knows? Maybe he legit didn't know. I mean, he said he liked history, but I think Madame A has been here since like the beginning of time. It's pretty awesome."

"Well, last night, Oliver acted like he had never heard of the Bone Artists," Dan pointed out. "And now this stuff with Finnoway? I feel like one of them is covering something up."

"Or both of them."

If those thugs—the Bone Artists—were still operating, then maybe that was what Micah had gotten wrapped up in. And if so, Dan really didn't like the idea of them holding on to his bones, planning to turn them into supposed magical talismans. Which led to his next question. "So, do they work?"

"What?" Jordan coughed on his tea.

"The bone talismans they were making. Were they just superstition, or did they really do something?"

Jordan put down his empty cup, worrying his lip piercing again. "I asked, but Madame A wouldn't answer," he whispered. "Frankly, I think that tells you everything you need to know."

Chapter 26

"*C*an we just talk about the fact that this Oliver bozo is definitely lying to us?" Jordan had maybe had a little too much of the sangria Uncle Steve had put out at dinner. He weaved as they walked the familiar route to Berkley & Daughters, gesturing wildly and colliding with Dan every few steps. "He lives here, right? He runs an antique shop. How could he not know about this bone-thingie legend?"

"I'm sure he has an explanation," Dan grumbled.

"Are you?" Abby had brought along their combined research—both the articles and pictures she had gathered on Jimmy Orsini and the papers Dan had collected about his parents. "I know he was Micah's friend, but that's not much to go on. If we can trust him, why would he give us only half the story?"

Dan wanted badly to answer, but there was nothing to say; his friends were right. Oliver and Sabrina owed them answers, and more than that, they owed him that box and whatever was inside it.

Berkley & Daughters sat shuttered and dark, but they were expected. Dan strode up to the door and went in without knocking, determined to show Oliver that he was leaving with that box, no matter what.

And then what?

The question haunted him as he stepped into the simmering candlelit darkness of the store.

"Really? Another séance?" Abby muttered. She sighed and skirted around Dan, then walked briskly to the counter, where Sabrina and Oliver were counting the cash register money and locking it away in a small deposit box.

"We need to talk," Dan said, following her.

Oliver shushed him. "Later."

"No, *now*."

"We're in the middle of something here," Sabrina whispered testily. "You can wait fifteen minutes, Crawford, it won't kill you."

"Trying to commune with your dear old granddad again?" Jordan slurred, not bothering to lower his voice. Dan winced.

"That's real sensitive of you. And no, for your information, we are not." But Oliver shifted uneasily; it was hard to tell in the low light, but he might have been blushing. "We're trying to reach Micah."

"Have you tried sending a text?" Jordan shot back.

"Would you just give it a rest? I know it might seem silly to you, but there are energies in this world, real, tangible energies that can be tapped into." Oliver disappeared into the back room for a moment to lock away the day's money. When he returned, he handed Dan a bowl. It smelled strongly of flowers.

"It's just rosewater," Oliver said in response to Dan's perplexed expression. "Dip your hands in and dry them off, then join us."

"That's not why we're here. We have questions for you," Abby replied. "We want Dan's box, and we want to know why you pretended not to know what the Bone Artists are."

"Look," Oliver said with a sigh, "you can have your goddamn box, all right? But Micah was reaching out to you, too, Dan. I want you sitting in on this with me."

It was a waste of time, but if fifteen minutes of playing along got him that box, Dan would do it. He flopped his hands around in the rosewater and then dried them on his T-shirt. Abby and Jordan stayed at the counter, watching, while Sabrina and Oliver escorted Dan to the round table in the corner.

He took one of the empty chairs, sitting between Sabrina and Oliver, looking down at the clean, white tablecloth and the strange symbol drawn across it. A handful of carved runes had been spread across the table, and a small basket with trinkets sat in the middle—a scrap of fabric, car keys, a curled-up canvas belt, and a picture of Micah and Oliver together as teenagers. Dan tore his eyes away from the photo. The two boys looked so happy, so innocent, arms around each other as they posed in front of Oliver's car. It was probably the day Oliver first got it, a monumental day in any boy's life.

Dan's hands were taken and grasped, then rested on the table. "What do I do?" he whispered.

The other people sitting around the table regarded him solemnly. There were seven of them, including Dan. One of the two girls to his right looked like she could be Sabrina's sister. The others he recognized from the séance he'd witnessed on the previous visit, including the woman with the ginger hair. He shuddered.

"Just close your eyes and focus on memories of him. If I sense his presence, I'll ask him where his bones are being kept," Oliver instructed. His hand was warm and slightly sweaty, but Sabrina's was cool in Dan's grasp.

As a last measure before they began, Oliver put his phone faceup on the table, perhaps thinking Micah might forego the usual shaking shutters and overturned chairs for more modern means of communication.

Dan inhaled deeply, preparing simply to sit and endure. For so long he had gone out of his way *not* to think about Micah or what had happened last fall; the further away it was, the easier it became. The warden, the Scarlets, Professor Reyes, Brookline . . . He had almost reached the point where he could live with the memories, and now he was being asked to bring it all back.

But thoughts of Micah came to him immediately. For a second, it felt as if the low, rhythmic chant of Oliver's voice asking for Micah's help was working like a spell, conjuring images of the school and the last seconds of Micah's life—the punishment he'd received for helping Dan escape. Despite the overabundance of candles in the room, Dan fought off a chill. The air in the room thinned, as if it were being sucked out by a vacuum. He felt something brush the back of his neck and gasped, convulsing, his eyes opening by sheer instinct.

His vision returned in time to see something silver shooting across the table toward him. Cold and final, it slammed into his eyeball, sending him toppling to the floor. He crashed with a shout, crumpling against the rickety chair back.

"Dan!"

Abby and Jordan were there, kneeling next to him while he frantically ran both hands over his face. There was nothing. No spike through his eye, no wound. Nothing.

"I felt . . . God, I could swear. . . ."

He rolled away from the chair and got to his knees, raising his head to meet the astonished gazes of Oliver and Sabrina.

"You felt it, too," Oliver said, nodding. "He was here."

"*Something* was here." He tried to catch his breath, tilting his head back and letting it fall loose on his neck. But something in the window caught his eye. The curtains had been pulled mostly shut, but in one small gap he noticed a face—a stark white face that made his blood run cold.

He had seen that face before, not in his nightmares but in photographs at the archives, at Uncle Steve's. . . .

"Something *is* here."

Oliver pulled back the curtain over the window, revealing a man whose face was hidden behind a crude rabbit mask. The candles in the window glinted off a sliver of silver in the rabbit-man's hand, a bone saw that glittered with a hundred sharp teeth.

Dan stumbled to his feet, shouting, but it was too late, the man was already sprinting away from the window, rushing to the door.

chapter
27

"The door!" Oliver screamed. "Brace the door!"

Dan and Jordan slammed into the door together just as the knob rattled and turned. The weight of one adult, then two, then three rocked back against them from the other side. Sabrina flew to the window, looking out into the street.

"Shit, there's too many of them!"

"How many?" Oliver shouted back. He had disappeared behind the counter, tossing first a hunting rifle and then a baseball bat to Abby.

"Six, I think," Sabrina called back.

"We can't hold them," Jordan grunted. Both he and Dan cried out as the back of a hammer cracked through the wood, showering them in splinters. "We really can't hold them!"

"Lock it and run!" Oliver vaulted over the counter, taking the rifle from Abby and leaving her with the bat. "Go! I'll hold them off while y'all get out the back."

Dan didn't need telling a second time. He had already thrown the deadbolt, but he jammed his hand against it again and turned the smaller lock on the knob, then grabbed Jordan and hauled him away from the door.

"Go!" Oliver took Sabrina by the arm and spun her around, pushing her toward the back door. She hesitated, but Abby pulled her through the curtain and into the storeroom. Fumbling for his phone, Dan managed to dial 911 with trembling fingers, his thumb hitting the call button just as the first rifle shot split the air.

"Who the hell was that?" Jordan yelled, following Sabrina, who had sprinted ahead to lead them safely through the side door. She ducked low as they ran, and the others did the same, flinching whenever another shot went off.

"I don't know," Sabrina replied. "Robbers ain't stupid enough to come this early in the night."

"Yes, I'd like to report a break-in," Dan barked into his phone. "In progress. The address? It's, um . . ." He tapped Sabrina on the shoulder and then thrust the phone into her hands. "Tell them where we are."

The second the phone was out of his hands, Dan felt his courage collapsing. What if they made it outside only to be attacked there? The police would take a while to get there, more than enough time for Oliver to run out of bullets. The gunfire was too loud, too jarring, the sound tearing through his body and making his teeth rattle.

Sabrina paused at the back door, finishing the call and handing Dan back his phone. "Quiet. Let me check if it's clear."

Behind him, he could hear one of the girls from the séance crying. It was too dark, and he couldn't see where the muffled little sobs were coming from. He could feel Jordan at his back and Abby ahead, tremors gripping her every few seconds while they waited for Sabrina's signal.

Then they were out, and while the open air felt less claustrophobic, it also felt more vulnerable.

"How many bullets are in that rifle?" Dan asked, shuffling over to the edge of the building. He peered into the alley, breathing a sigh of relief when he found it empty. "We have to go back and help him somehow."

"No, no way," Jordan whispered, frantic. "I vote for run like hell."

"Jordan's right. What are we going to do with a baseball bat?"

"We can't just leave him!"

Oh God, it was like Micah's death all over again. Oliver wasn't going to make it, and Dan would spend the rest of his life with the man's death on his hands. Why did history keep repeating itself?

Maybe the others would run, but Dan was sick and tired of feeling hunted. He darted down the alley, not knowing or caring if his friends were following. There was no plan, not yet, but a plan would come when he saw what was left of the store. Sirens whined and grew louder, screaming in from the street to the right. The cops had mercifully arrived quicker than he'd thought. Clinging to the brick wall, Dan listened to the rifle shots cease, shortly followed by the sound of pounding footsteps.

That's when he saw them: six masked figures, all sprinting across the avenue to the opposite sidewalk, and from there into a narrow alley.

Screw the plan. Keeping his distance, Dan chased after.

Chapter

28

*I*t wasn't until he careened into the far alley that he heard footsteps at his back. Jordan and Abby. He pushed his legs harder, running after the masked attackers before they could fade into the crowded gloom of one of the main streets. They were at least four blocks from Oliver's shop now, and Dan was gaining on them as quickly as he dared. He waited behind a Dumpster until he felt certain they were too far ahead to notice him. That was when Abby and Jordan caught up.

"Are you crazy? You can't take these people on." Jordan made a grab for Dan's sleeve, but he dodged.

"I'm not trying to fight them, Jordan. I'm not an idiot. I just want to see where they go."

"Why? So you can go back later and get yourself killed then?"

"No, so I can figure out who the hell they are." Dan wasn't going to argue and he wasn't going to raise his voice and risk being seen. He broke into a run again, modulating his speed to try to keep at least a block between him and his targets.

They vanished around a corner, and when Dan turned it, slowly, carefully, he found himself at a fork in the alley, where an ancient grate in the cobblestone road vented a plume of steam. Dan swore under his breath, checking down both potential escape routes. They were short lanes, and already empty. A few ambient footsteps echoed down from the right fork, and he veered that way, hoping he'd made the right call.

The short alley branch dumped him out onto a wide, two-lane road, one that was well kept and tourist friendly. A bright café sat across the street, its doors closed for the night but a string of fat Christmas bulbs still twinkling in the window. He listened again for the footsteps, trying to ignore the sound of Abby and Jordan gasping for air behind him.

He hooked around the slender, two-story building that housed the café. Dan drew up short just as he rounded the corner, peering down a new alley to see the last of the figures pulling off his mask and ducking into a side door. A ragged canvas awning hung over the door, protecting what looked like a downward staircase that led into the building's basement.

"Gotcha," Dan murmured. He wiped blindly at the sweat on his forehead, not noticing until then that his shirt was soaked through.

Jordan and Abby caught up to him again, and he motioned for them to be silent, pointing to the door to indicate where the people had gone inside.

"I hope you realize how lucky you are," Jordan whispered. "What is this place?"

Dan waited a few seconds, until he was sure that the people weren't immediately coming back out. Hopefully they were in the clear now.

"Let's find out," he whispered back.

He walked slowly out into the alley. The front of the building looked completely out of place in the ugly alley; the façade was recently power washed and pristine, painted a bright, chalky white.

Beside the staircase down to the basement, a three-step walk-up led to a silver door. Dan took out his phone and snapped a picture, then dropped a pin on his map app so he could save the address. Next to the silver door, a sign advertising Rampart Street Funerary Home had fallen at an angle, a huge For Sale sticker tacked to the bottom.

Who knew how long that sticker had been there. Clearly, this funerary home was still in business.

Chapter 29

*D*an's phone buzzed twice in his pocket, breaking the paralysis that had descended over all three of them as they neared the safer part of town close to Uncle Steve's apartment. Dan was relieved to find they were texts from Sabrina.

"Funerary home, Dan. Bodies, Dan. *Bones*, Dan."

"Yes, thank you, Jordan, I know," Dan said, locking eyes with him.

"No, I mean seriously. What the hell? Tell me we are not being followed by freaky bone doctors."

"Sabrina says Oliver is okay, in case you were wondering. Just shaken up, and he might have dislocated his shoulder firing the rifle so much," Dan reported. His hands were still shaking, but at least none of them had gotten hurt.

"Screw them. We were attacked by masked crazies because we were at that damn store. There's no way that's a coincidence!" Jordan sliced his hand through the air, but Abby remained silent, still clutching her files. "And God! What if they track this back to us through Oliver and Sabrina? This shit with them has got to stop. They are nice but toxic."

"They were attacked, too," Dan pointed out quickly. "And it's Oliver's shop that got the worst of it."

"Yes. Exactly. Oliver's shop. None of this terrible crap started

happening until we met those two! From now on we are staying far, far away from them. The councilman tried to warn you,
Dan. They're bad news. I don't know if they're bad luck or into
some bad stuff or have bad juju or what, but I'm done." With that,
they lapsed into silence again.

Dan didn't expect Abby to come to his side. He wasn't even sure
he had a side. Was it Oliver they'd wanted or him? That was maybe
the only thing he knew for sure—that one of them was the target.
Sweaty, miserable, and still trembling, he glanced surreptitiously
at his friends; yet again he had gotten them in danger. Maybe it
was time to follow Jordan's advice and cut Oliver and Sabrina out
of his life.

But they still have that box.

Damn it. Would one more day really make the difference?
He could go alone to Oliver's shop and get the box, say his
good-byes, and that would be that. At least then he would feel
like less of a coward for leaving Oliver to deal with Micah's
relentless messages alone, when Dan had had way more to do
with Micah's death than Oliver had.

Dan felt exhaustion dragging his head down as they finally
reached Uncle Steve's block. Police sirens blipped and chirped,
blue and red lights reflecting in alternating patterns along the
buildings. At first, Dan assumed they were just holdovers from
the break-in at Oliver's, but the lights weren't going anywhere.
The trio circled back to approach the building from the north,
watching traffic clog the road as everyone tried to maneuver
around the police cars parked on the sidewalk.

"No," he heard Jordan murmur. "No, that's not his house.
It can't be his house."

Jordan pushed Dan and Abby aside, darting between them and sprinting down the sidewalk. Three police cars vied for space in front of Uncle Steve's door, and worse, an ambulance was parked just a few yards away. Exhaustion forgotten, Dan ran after his friend, Abby close behind.

"Dan, if anything's happened to him . . ." She grabbed Dan's wrist hard and squeezed.

"God, I know. What do we do?"

"Just stay strong for Jordan. That's probably the only thing we can do."

"That's my uncle!" Jordan was shouting. One of the officers had intervened to keep him from crossing the flimsy barricade of police tape. "Let me through! That's my uncle and I want to see him!"

Abby tried a different tactic, calmly putting a hand on Jordan's shoulder and smiling up at the police officer. "Can you tell us what happened, officer? We're staying with Steve Lipcott. Our things are inside if you need to verify that."

The officer, a short, stocky man with a sallow complexion and beady eyes, stared at them for a long moment from under his cap. He scribbled something on the clipboard in his hands and then nodded to the space behind him. "You'll have to wait a moment. Can't let you through without checking that out."

"Of course," Abby said, using that same calm voice. "We understand."

"No, we don't!" Jordan shrieked. "Is he okay? Jesus, just tell me if my uncle's okay!"

"He's fine. A little roughed up, but he'll make it. Ambulance is taking him to Ochsner Baptist. You can get a lift over

there after answering a few questions, all right?"

That was enough to keep Jordan from barreling through the police tape. They watched the stretcher with Steve's blanketed and still form being popped into the ambulance. Abby and Dan put their arms around their friend.

"I'm so sorry, Jordan," Dan murmured. The knot in his stomach told him this was his fault. It seemed like the worst possible answer to his question—apparently, he and Oliver were *both* targets.

"Don't talk to me right now. Just don't say a word, okay?" Jordan shied away from Dan's arm, so Dan let it drop.

"You can't blame Dan for this," Abby said softly.

"Oh really? I can't? Watch me."

"Jordan—"

"You better hope this doesn't have anything to do with your stupid new friends," Jordan added in a vicious whisper. "Or those bone artists will be nothing compared to what I do to you."

"Dan, he doesn't mean that." Abby turned to him with a sad half smile, one he couldn't return.

"Yes, I do."

Rolling his eyes in disgust, Dan left his friends huddling beside the police tape, waiting for the officer to question them. He walked over to an empty space on the sidewalk and sat down hard on the pavement, letting his head droop low over his knees. Not for the first time in their short, intense friendship, Dan wondered if his friends were about to turn on him.

Jordan's words echoed like gunshots in his head.

He wanted to get up and leave, wander, let Jordan cool off, and hope that he realized Dan never wished anything but the best for them, even if he often ended up bringing about the worst. What had Jordan called Sabrina and Oliver? Nice but toxic? Wasn't that so like Dan, too?

Sighing, he rested his chin on the back of his hands and gazed out blindly at the street. The clouds hanging over the city felt ready to burst, and the tension of it resonated in his back. His meandering attention fell on the building opposite Uncle Steve's, landing on a smear of white paint. Something winked at him from memory, an image that almost went unremembered in his exhaustion. Hadn't there been graffiti on that wall when they arrived?

Standing, he glanced to see if his friends were still on the sidewalk, then he jogged across the traffic-clogged street, inspecting the smudgy white stain left behind on the bricks. He touched it lightly, his fingers coming away with a gritty residue. It wasn't paint at all, but some kind of heavy chalk. He remembered a skull there and some French phrase, though he couldn't conjure the exact words. He shivered, thinking of that stark, white rabbit face staring at him through the window.

"Dan! Dan, what's going on? The police need to talk to us!" Abby called at him from across the street, waving frantically.

He nodded and backed slowly away from the wall, reaching into his pocket for his phone. He started a new text to Oliver, feeling a lump of anxiety grow in his throat.

"*I need you to check something,*" he wrote. "*Look across the street. What do you see?*"

"Rooms were tossed, but just the one laptop was taken. No jewelry, no other electronics—not even the other computer. Care to tell us what was on that laptop?"

Dan's knee bounced compulsively as he sat in the hospital waiting room. A hand grabbed him by the thigh, stopping his leg; he had been shaking the entire bank of chairs. Abby's dark, drawn face blinked back at him as he fought the grip of her hand for a second. Then he let his leg relax.

"What are you thinking?" Abby asked quietly. A policeman was still with them, distracted with his phone in the corner of the room while they waited on news of Uncle Steve's condition.

Jordan was a wreck, pacing nonstop, crushing a soda can in his hand. Dan could hear the quiet *scrape-scrape-scrape* as Jordan worried his lip piercing with his tongue. The sound gnawed at him, dry and clacking.

"You know what I'm thinking." Dan let his eyes slide from the ceiling to her wan face. "They took the laptop with Jordan's emails to Maisie."

"I don't understand any of this." She sighed and rubbed at her eyes, smudging her eye makeup until it looked like she'd been crying. "The important thing is, Jordan will come around. Deep down he knows this isn't your fault, but right now he just needs someone to lash out at, someone to blame." She put a comforting hand on Dan's back, rubbing his shoulders. "Give him time."

"I plan to." He leaned into her hand, finding it the only thing that kept him from tearing his hair out completely. "And I also plan to get some answers."

"I don't like the sound of that," she said. "What do you mean?"

"Think about it. Maisie Moore shared those articles about my parents, and then gets hit by a car and killed. My parents were arrested for messing around in some company's secret affairs, then they die in a car wreck, too. Now, in the same night that the Bone Artists try to kill us at Oliver's shop, Uncle Steve gets attacked. We're not the only ones trying to tie up loose ends, Abby. For those guys, we *are* the loose ends." He straightened his back, watching Jordan's feet go back and forth across the linoleum.

"Dan . . ."

Scrape–scrape–scrape.

"I won't do anything reckless," he said.

"Make that a promise and I'll feel a lot better."

Dan swiveled to meet her eyes, feeling her hand go still on his back. She really was so beautiful to him, and feeling her there next to him, long-suffering and understanding, made it that much harder to say the next two words.

"I promise."

Scrape–scrape–scrape.

The door to Uncle Steve's room opened and a harried-looking nurse appeared. She gave Jordan a careful smile and gestured to the room behind her. "You can go in now, but he needs his rest."

Jordan barreled past her and Abby stood.

"Coming?" she asked.

"Just after I make a quick phone call. I want to let Paul and Sandy know what happened."

It was the second lie he had told in as many minutes.

Chapter 30

The thick metal instrument scraped across his teeth. The sound echoed deafeningly in his head, like the rasp of a file across steel. He couldn't close his mouth or move his head; something held his mouth open so wide it felt like his jaw would pop and break if pushed another centimeter. Helpless. Trapped. His eyes rolled back, the tension in his head spreading to the rest of his prone body. Then there came a tugging, hard and insistent, and he felt the first tooth tear away and the fast gush of pain and blood that followed, flooding his mouth with copper.

A speed bump knocked him out of the dream. How had he fallen asleep over such a short car ride? He must have been more exhausted than he realized. The pain lingered, and he grabbed his jaw, running his tongue anxiously around his teeth. All there. Still, it filled him with a second's hesitation.

Then he realized the cabbie was staring at him.

"Uh, hello? You gonna tell me where to go next or just hope that I'm a mind reader?"

Dan shook the phone out of his pocket, opening the GPS again to zero in on their location.

"Right. Sorry. You want a left here, then three more blocks down Rampart. It should be on the right."

He had waited until Jordan and Abby were both passed out cold in Steve's hospital room. They were curled up like puppies on the shallow chairs in there, and Dan had slinked away while he could, watching early morning shock the city awake with an orange and purple sky.

Now the cab rolled down the sleepy city block, slowing and slowing until the tires squeaked. Dan leaned into the window, another spasm of fear tightening his stomach, making him reconsider his present course.

Oliver hadn't responded to his text from the night before, but there was no telling what had happened after the police arrived. He and Sabrina were probably busy trying to clean up the mess at the store. Either way, Dan had made his decision. There was something hidden in that old funeral home, and he wanted to know what it was.

"Thanks," he said, shoving a fistful of cash at the driver. "You don't have to wait."

Outside on the curb, a final instinctive urge told him to tell someone, anyone, where he had gone.

"Hey," he texted Oliver. He was the one with the gun, after all, and he was one of the few people who wouldn't be mad at Dan upon receipt of this message. Dan sent his present address and a word that he was pretty sure he knew who was responsible for trashing the store, and he was at their base now.

He checked up and down the street, half for masked lunatics waiting to ambush him and half for any random excuse not to go inside.

The coast was clear.

He didn't exactly have Jordan's skills with breaking and entering, but hanging out with him had given him a few tricks. The door at the bottom of the steps was locked, but there was a window a little ways down that looked flimsy, and it appeared to connect to the same room. Dan went over to a pile of fruit crates that had been left out with a heap of garbage in the alley, and he tore off a wooden slat, returning to jam the thin piece of wood under the window frame. At first the window wouldn't budge, but after a few sharp jabs, the board dug into the gap, and just as he hoped, the crossbar on the inside was rotted and soft. With a few more punches down on the slat, the window jumped free and he was able to push it open the rest of the way.

He checked one more time up and down the alley. A single cat watched him from a fence separating the back of the building from the others behind it. But even the cat didn't seem much interested in what he was doing. Dan swiveled, knocking the window screen into the room with one hard kick. But in so doing, he lost his balance, toppling inside and swallowing a panicky shriek as he fell into what felt like a bin full of old bath towels.

He popped up, gracelessly rolling out of the bin and onto the floor. Frantic, he beat at his arms, dust flying off his sleeves in choking clouds. The giant box he'd fallen into spilled over with old velvet cloths that looked like table runners, most likely decorations for the caskets or altars. Nothing strange about that. In fact, nothing at all about the large, open room he had fallen into seemed strange. It was only slightly lower than street level, with cobwebbed chandeliers and the kind of classic, sophisticated paneling and trim that recalled the old world. He could just imagine the hundreds, maybe thousands, of families that had come and gone through here over the years, grieving and saying final words. Dark stripes on the floor indicated where the rows of benches had been for mourners, and the carpet

walkway that had led to the casket was still there, though now badly in need of vacuuming and slightly askew.

The dirty windows allowed in just enough light for him to safely navigate the halls to the other rooms. He went right, following a thin corridor toward the back of the building. The only other way would be to go down to the front foyer, which seemed to be the path to the main door. He stepped lightly, wary of the creaking floorboards. The building had been abandoned for years, judging by the thick clumps of dust that flew up in his wake and shivered down from the walls just from the light breeze of his passing.

At the end of the corridor, an open door waited.

Dan paused in the frame, taking in the floor-to-ceiling wooden cabinets of an office. An imposing wooden desk stretched across most of the floor, long-abandoned cushioned chairs left in their original positions. This could have been where the owners arranged the services and sold the caskets. It was strange that the furniture remained. The desk was heavy, sure, but probably worth moving if it could be sold to an antique dealership.

That thought, however, quickly fled as he felt an eerie chill coalesce behind him. It wasn't just a random air duct coming to life, but a concentration of cold energy. He turned, feeling his heart convulse and freeze and then pump again. His mouth hung open a little as he came face-to-face one more time with his father.

But Marcus didn't notice him. He passed through Dan like a sigh, striding quickly into the office. Dan turned and watched, transfixed, as the shape of his father attacked drawer after drawer. The drawers in the present didn't react, but clearly Marcus had been searching for something.

"You're sure it's here, Evie?" he said, the dark baritone of his voice tinged on the edges with odd reverberation. The words echoed within themselves, somehow, as if straining to travel through time to Dan. "Just help me look, Goddamn it! We don't have time."

Then he paused, standing from where he had been kneeling to inspect a cabinet, and turned toward something or someone. Marcus hugged what should have been another body, but was simply air. "I didn't mean to shout at you. That was . . . This whole mess just has me on edge. Promise me we can leave. Promise me we can get out of town once you're satisfied."

His father leaned in to kiss someone, smiling sadly, and then went back to searching the cabinet drawers. Dan inched closer, wanting to see his father up close, wanting to confirm he was really seeing this. No quick blip of the mind could do this. It was so clear, clearer and crisper than any vision he had stumbled into before. Maybe because it was more recent than the moment in the Arlington School, or because the connection was that much stronger here. He didn't understand it, but he watched, his chest tight with loss.

"You found it? Oh, thank God. Show me. . . ." Marcus whirled around, crossing to the other side of the office. Dan watched his father reach for a specific row of cabinets and yank at the handle. "The label's worn off, but this has to be right. Wait. What was that? Did you hear that? Evie, we have to go. Just . . . Damn it, Evie! Leave it! We don't have time!"

And he could swear his father—no more corporeal than blue smoke, but still his father—turned and looked him directly in the eye. "We have to leave. There's no time!"

Just like before, he vanished as abruptly as he had appeared. Dan shivered, frightened by the thought that he could conjure those memories just by walking in the right place at the right time. But last time his father had shown him something—maybe this time it would work, too.

His hand trembled as he pulled open the last cabinet Marcus had touched. Alphabetized folder tabs sprung up, aged but legible. They fluttered softly as he ran his hand over them. He flipped through the tabs, stopping at *ARMAINE—ASPEN*.

One folder stuck up at a funny angle, never quite pushed all the way back down after his mother had tried to take it. Just like his father had said, the label was missing, leaving it anonymous but for the doodle someone had drawn in pen on the outside. It looked like a squished smiley face.

Dan glanced through the open doorway that led back to the corridor. Still alone. He quickly grabbed the folder, trying to decide whether to take it and go or read it right there. His curiosity got the better of him, and he pulled out the top sheets. They were funeral arrangements, all for various people named Ash. The first few were all people who'd been born in the sixties, which could easily have made them members of his mother's immediate family. Maybe sisters, a cousin . . . God. All of them dead, most within a few years of one another, between 1990 and 1995. The funeral director had scribbled notes about the deceased—*automobile accident, automobile accident, accidental drowning, drug overdose. . . .*

While suggestive, it didn't explain anything for sure. It didn't *prove* anything. There had to be something he wasn't seeing. Dan kept looking further back through the Ash family

records, trying to spot anomalies, and when that turned up nothing, trying to spot similarities.

And then he saw it.

In the most recent deaths, the funeral director had arranged for the remains to be picked up and transferred to the building. The driver dispatched to the locations was the same every time.

Stanton Finnoway.

A brother? A cousin? It didn't matter.

"I knew it," Dan whispered, taking the papers and folding them messily. "That bastard."

A single footfall creaked down the hall.

Chapter 31

"*N*ame-calling? Really?"

Why had Dan thought he had more time? Hadn't his father warned him to leave? The footstep he'd heard belonged to Tamsin. Finnoway was already there, just behind him. Dan was cornered and outnumbered, and reasonably confident that the councilman could outmatch him in a fight.

He backed into the cabinet, closing it as he went.

"Is there a reason you're trespassing on my property?" the councilman asked, his eyes going at once to the papers folded up in Dan's hand. "Or just out for a stroll?"

"There's no way to make this look better, is there?" Dan tried to gauge his chances of making a dash for the door. Tamsin wasn't exactly brawny, but she also seemed like the type to carry a weapon.

"No, there really isn't." Finnoway nodded toward Dan's hand and the old records tucked away in it. "I assume you think you've found something important. That's actually touching. I'm touched in this moment. Do you know why?"

"I couldn't care less," Dan muttered. He could try to inch his way around the room and circle, but that would take forever. Maybe Oliver would come looking for him, but that seemed like a distant possibility. He couldn't count on anyone but himself in this godforsaken town.

"I'm touched because you *were* on the cusp of something," Finnoway explained, gesturing Tamsin forward. He was wearing a long, light coat, one that looked like it could conceal any number of small weapons. Smiling, he snapped his fingers. Gloved fingers, Dan noticed—gloves made of sleek, black leather. "So close. Am I right? You had the most peculiar look on your face when you turned around just now. Wonderment and then—like that—*terror*. That's where the real discoveries lie."

The heat and color drained from Dan's face.

"Tamsin, if you would please."

She was faster than Dan could have predicted, striking like a coiled snake, lunging over Finnoway's shoulder with a tiny, flashing needle. Before Dan could respond, he felt a light pricking sensation in his neck.

He had enough time to spin and see the assistant's bloodred lips curl into a smile. Then the floor was right at his back, his chin, hitting him like a full-bodied punch. He couldn't stop staring at the assistant's shoes. They were so, so pointy. . . .

"Not a bad find," he heard Finnoway rumble, the darkness suddenly acute and nauseating, tar thick and drowning him. "But not enough to wipe away the boy's debt."

Chapter

32

*H*e dipped into consciousness twice. The first time was when the first commotion started, a door banging open, startling him enough that he could open his eyes and see, briefly, blurred images of a stark white wall and a faceless face, lit from behind by a strong, white light. The air smelled strongly of antiseptic and underneath that, mint, stirring memories of childhood fears.

"I can't believe I missed this. Another Ash. This should've been taken care of years ago. But it's never too late to tie up loose ends."

Then another face appeared, this one shinier and larger than the others. Looking at it was like staring into a void—no, a black, glittering orb like a starry sky—and then the face turned into a person and the person was breathing hard, carrying him. . . . Deep-sea noises surrounded him and then a dark, masculine voice made him shrivel up inside his skin.

"What the hell is this? Who are you? Stop him!"

The overwhelming nausea forced him back to sleep.

The second time he woke up, two familiar faces swam in front of his eyes. It took a frighteningly long time to discern any more than that, his head swaying back and forth as he tried to concentrate.

"I think he's waking up." It was Oliver's voice, and the familiarity of it made Dan want to burst into tears. He was safe. Thank God he was safe. His hand ached like crazy, but at least he was no longer in Finnoway's clutches.

Oliver's familiar dark eyes came into focus; the other boy was kneeling next to the mattress on which Dan lay. Oliver put one hand on Dan's shoulder, shaking gingerly. His eyes were huge, searching back and forth across Dan's face. "I know you're still weak, but I need you to try and remember."

"Remember what?" Dan growled. Ugh. His throat felt like it had been rubbed with rocks. "Where am I?"

"You're at my apartment and safe. Everything's going to be okay, I just need you to think back. He must have said something. He had to say the words. Was our debt repaid? Was *my* debt repaid?"

Dan's head swam as he tried to make sense of the question. His memories had fractured, and for the moment he could do nothing but blink back at the other boy. "I don't understand. . . . Oliver, you saved me. You . . . I don't know what that evil asshole would've done to me. He drugged me and then . . . I don't remember much. I don't remember *anything*."

"You don't?" Oliver sat back on his heels, then leapt to his feet and began pacing back and forth. "No, that's not right. He *had* to say the words. This should've been enough. You should have been enough."

Enough? Dan blinked up at him through foggy eyes. His shirt smelled strangely minty, like he had just been to the dentist's office. Just following Oliver's path back and forth across the room made Dan dizzy again. "Oliver . . . What are you talking about?"

Stopping dead in his tracks, Oliver spun to face him, wringing his hands out and then approaching again to fall to his knees. "Dan. I messed up."

Flashes of the morning returned to him. Images in reverse. He felt the heat of the needle pricking his neck, then the cold shiver of his father's ghost walking through him. A Finnoway's name on those funeral documents. Documents, he was now certain, that were gone.

Not a bad find. But not enough to wipe away the debt.

"I don't understand. You saved me," Dan murmured, curling up on himself in the bed.

"I wish that was true." But it clearly wasn't. Dan recoiled, no longer trusting the safety that Oliver had mentioned. Had he tumbled from one fire and into another? "But I didn't realize how stupid I'd been until you turned up unconscious on my stoop. I was grateful that you were alive. No, that's a lie. I was afraid. But now I'm grateful."

It was still like Oliver was speaking in another language altogether, and Dan's head was too stuffed with cotton to make sense of the words. "Wait—I 'turned up'?"

"Yeah, some good Samaritan was kind enough to dump your ass on my doorstep, out cold and bandaged. Not exactly a delivery I was expecting." Oliver smoothed both hands over his face, scrubbing at his forehead.

"Who, though?" Dan murmured. "Who would come for me and then just leave?"

"I don't know who did it, but you owe them a debt of gratitude for damn sure," Oliver said. "Most people, they tangle with Finnoway and they don't make it out alive."

"How do you know that?" Dan replied gruffly. He was still trying to wrap his head around the phrase "out cold and bandaged," but he was getting the clear impression that his friends had been right about Oliver after all. "Bandaged," he whispered, unsteady against the pillows.

"Yeah," Oliver said softly, carefully picking up Dan's hand and lifting it so Dan could see it. His hand was wrapped tightly in a bulky bandage, clean and white, secured over the palm with a tiny metal clip. His bright pink fingers poked out of the bandage, except for one.

Where his little finger should have been was just a blank. He gaped at the empty spot, feeling that throb from before return and spread, searing down toward his elbow.

They have my bones.

Chapter

33

"*He* took it."

Oliver didn't respond, and if Dan had been any stronger in that moment, he would've lurched out of bed to shake him.

The room above the shop in which Oliver apparently lived was cramped and low ceilinged, with only one grimy window that faced out into the alley. The walls in here were crammed with bookcases, each shelf overflowing more than the last. Outside, it had begun to rain, the droplets pattering on the window in a soothing crescendo as the wind picked up and carried them harder against the building. A few naked lightbulbs swung from the ceiling, and black-and-white pictures of people Dan didn't recognize hung on the walls. Oliver's family, maybe. Some of the shots looked old enough to be from the start of the store.

"Listen, Dan. I'm gonna say some things right now that you're not gonna like. I just need you to listen and then hate me afterward, all right?"

Dan shook under the blankets. He didn't want to listen. He had to, but he didn't want to. There was no processing what he was looking at on his hand, and Oliver's words at least distracted him from the fact that he would really have to confront it eventually.

"Here's the box you wanted," Oliver said, moving to sit on a rickety wooden chair next to the bed. "But it's not entirely what I said it was."

Oliver cleared his throat and swung into a more upright sitting position. At his feet, a cardboard storage box waited, tattered, stained, and empty.

When Oliver tried to offer him a mug of tea from the side table, Dan refused to take it. He didn't want anything from Oliver now. He had wanted the box, sure, but now it was clear that the box had been some kind of trick.

"There's nothing in it," Dan said, dragging his eyes from the box to Oliver. "Is this a joke?"

"There *was* a box, Dan, but you need to let me explain."

"Do I?" He laughed, dry and sarcastic, and rolled his eyes to the ceiling. "I guess I do, since I'm not sure my legs even work at this point. They're still there though, right?"

"He just took the finger."

"Why? Why only that?"

Oliver stared back evenly, moistening his lips before saying, "Because that's all he needs. It depends. . . . Sometimes we take a lot more than a finger, but there's always a reason. We don't usually know the reason, but Finnoway does."

"*We?*"

"Yes, we, Dan. That's part of what I'm trying to tell you. I got chumped into working for the Bone Artists, just like I said. But I never stopped working for them, not really. The story I told you . . . There were a few inventions in there."

Dan pulled his knees up toward his chest, using his left arm to try to help them along. He'd have to get used to avoiding his right hand for a while. Just looking at it now made his stomach somersault, and as the feeling in his limbs started to come back, the pain was already immense. "I'm too sedated at the moment to smack you, so please, keep taking advantage of that."

"No smacking necessary," Oliver said, putting up his hands in surrender. "You can't make me feel worse than I already do. Not that it's much help to you now."

"Jordan told me not to trust you. Man, he had your number from day one."

"You still don't understand. This isn't about me. Or not just me. This started with our families. My granddad, your parents. They were all wanted for messing with the Bone Artists, and the Bone Artists never let a grudge go unless the debt is repaid. I tried to get out of the debt by doing the petty work with Micah, and when they wanted me to start stealing bones, I really did try to quit. But Finnoway wouldn't let me."

Dan remained silent, hoping that if he just waited long enough, the nightmare would end, and he'd be back at Uncle Steve's in a warm, safe bed with a plate of beignets and all ten of his fingers.

"What debt did you owe, exactly?"

Oliver nodded to one of the photos hanging behind Dan. "You see that statue? It's in a park not six blocks from here. It's my grandfather, Edmund Berkley. He was a shopkeep, then a lawyer, then one of the fairest damn judges you ever seen. This town loved him, and they loved him even more when he finally cleaned up Jimmy Orsini and his smuggling, thieving, low-life friends."

The name drew Dan further out of his grogginess. He sat up straighter.

"My grandfather was on the right side of the law on that fight. Jimmy didn't live out his last days in jail like he was supposed to. He died after being rescued and gunned down, and that was just fine by most of the law-abiding folks around here."

"I've heard that story," Dan said, and Oliver's eyebrows shot up. "Abby's been researching Orsini for part of her photo project. We even found an old article about him in Shreveport that had that creepy Bone Artist poem on it."

Oliver sighed and scratched his chin, pointing to the picture with the statue of his grandfather again. "I don't know if he ever suspected just how deep the well ran with Jimmy. Jimmy was an old man by the time my grandfather put him away, but he was one of the originals. Hell, he might have been *the* Prince of the Body Thieves in the damn poem. Point is, he wasn't just running gin and drugs, he was dealing in human bones, too. Thought they were magic."

Dan nodded slowly. "That's what Madame A told Jordan. I suspect you know more about them than she does."

"Way more. More than I'd like."

"So what, your granddad got Orsini put in jail, so the rest of the Bone Artists came after him?" Dan said. "What the hell does that have to do with my parents?"

"The Bone Artists are like the mob, a family business. They ran booze and drugs down here before, and they'll run it down here forever. It ain't just a bunch of gangsters anymore, they're organized, and like I said, they hold a grudge." Oliver reached under his chair, pulling out a half-empty bottle of rum. He swigged from it, then wiped his mouth with the back of his hand. "They're gonna finish wiping out my whole family for what my grandfather did, and now they're gonna wipe out all of yours for what your mother did."

"What my . . ." Dan lapsed into silence. *Of course.* What had Maisie Moore called Trax Corp. in her article? A modern smuggling ring? Dan's mother had uncovered a company that had been moving untested drugs out of the South and into New England for years. Into Brookline, back when the warden was there. But she hadn't just pissed off a corrupt corporation. She'd pissed off a powerful, secret cult.

Dan couldn't speak for a moment; his wires were too crossed. For a year, he'd thought his blood was poison—that the tainted Crawford legacy that had been passed down to him from the warden had doomed him for life. Now, he realized the same was true about the Ash side of the family.

"So your dad—when Sabrina said he was killed by a drunk driver . . . ?" Dan asked, studying the boy closely.

"I don't know how a drunk man gets all the way across that causeway safely, then suddenly, bam, decides to veer into the next lane. But it was a hit-and-run. Hard to pin that on anyone, you hear what I'm saying? Same goes for a couple on the run that just takes a dive off a cliff in the family car." He said this with a straight, dark look into Dan's face.

My parents were murdered. Even though part of him had suspected it earlier, internalizing that horrible fact was a different matter entirely. It was like accepting the fact that he had lost a finger.

But anger soon replaced despair. "You *knew* all of this? And what was I, the bait?" He held up his bandaged hand, shoving it in Oliver's face. "This happened because of you!"

Gently shaking his head, Oliver pushed Dan's hand away.

"When I first heard from Micah that you could help me, I thought maybe you had some information I could use to pay my debt. Or at least trade up, like Micah did. I found your tent right where Micah said it would be, except I had second thoughts about dragging you into all this. Then you came into my shop that first night, and you said your name was Dan Crawford. Well, it rang a bell. I'd just seen the box in the shop storage, *CRAWFORD & ASH*. That night, I got curious."

Oliver stood and snatched up the rum bottle, turning it this way and that, studying the well-worn label peeling off the glass. "We all know what families are on the list—what debts the Bone Artists still want to collect on. Ash is one of those families. And I'm sorry, but you'd just told me Micah was dead and you didn't have jack to help me. Once I figured out that you were the son of Evelyn Ash, and here my dad had had this box of her stuff to boot, well. You were my last hope of getting out. Now it's over for me."

Dan wanted to spring out of the bed. Hit him. Kill him. He could hardly move, paralyzed by the knowledge that all this—Maisie Moore's death, Steve being attacked, *Dan's lost finger*—was because Oliver had turned him in.

"Do you realize how selfish and *cruel* you are?"

Oliver stared at him with wide, haunted eyes. He looked at the floor and then at Dan's bandaged hand. "I see that now. I thought one stranger was fair trade for my life back. But you're not a stranger anymore." Oliver's eyes welled up with tears, but then he swallowed them down until his eyes looked vacant. "Anyway, even after you, Finnoway didn't clear my debt, and he never will. I'm so *damn* sorry, Dan. I betrayed Micah, I betrayed my father's trust, and I betrayed you. There's nothing I can do except promise to try and make this right."

"Make it right?" Dan couldn't catch his breath. Oliver had planned to trade him in—like a bargaining chip! And now he just wanted to apologize?

Dan rolled onto his back, staring blankly up at the ceiling. *And wouldn't you have done the same thing last summer, if it meant getting out from under the shadow of the warden's legacy? Even now, what if you could trade one person to escape the nightmares—Brookline, the Scarlets, and now the Bone Artists?*

He would. He knew he would. Oliver's choice, though Dan would never agree with it, at least began to make a horrifying kind of sense. It wasn't fair or right, but counting a stranger's worth over his own family's? It was an impossible situation.

"It's funny. Finnoway warned me about you, too." Dan's voice was raw, but he had to say it.

"Probably meant it in earnest. The man's a monster, but a monster with a code." Oliver too sounded hoarse and exhausted. "He had no idea who or what you were until I told him. And then this morning, when you texted me about going to the funeral home. I told him exactly where you were."

"Well, I made it out alive. That's something. I can work with that."

"There's something else."

Jordan's prophetic words leapt to mind. *There always is.*

"Dare I ask?" Dan wasn't sure how much more he could stand to have dumped in his lap. Oliver had already unloaded plenty.

"We need to get your finger back." A dark shadow passed over Oliver's face. His boyish features hardened, a tendon working in his jaw. "If it doesn't end up as a talisman, it will end up as something else. Finnoway is too smart. There's a reason he took what he did."

There was no stopping Dan's outraged guffaw. *"Get it back?* How do you foresee us doing that? And anyway, the damage is done. It's not like a doctor can sew it back on at this point."

"Think, Dan. Think about Micah."

"What, you think they're using Micah's skeleton to send us the messages? And now they're going to use my finger bones to, I don't know, haunt a mitten? The talisman thing is just a legend. A spooky story for kids. Even Finnoway said so."

"Finnoway sold you a lie, just like I did. That's what we do." Oliver vented a bitter chuckle and drank from the rum bottle. "These people will get at you any way they can. They don't just have your bones, they have a fingerprint, blood, DNA. . . . Even if all the rest of it is just legend, your flesh and blood aren't. I've never seen a talisman made—I'm not that important—but they *are* made and they *do* work. I know that much."

Dan sighed, thinking of Professor Reyes and her obsession with Maudire's crystal necklace. *Stranger things*, he mused dryly. "I guess I have to believe you, even if I really, *really* don't want to." He dropped his forehead into his left palm. "So how do I get it back?"

"I don't rightly know," Oliver muttered, turning away. "But sooner is better than later."

"I agree. But first, I know two people who are probably very worried about me right about now."

Chapter 34

"We have to go to the police with this."

On the plus side, Jordan was talking to him again, but Dan suspected that had a lot to do with his missing finger. Before leaving Oliver's he had taken off the bandage and, cringing, discovered that while his stomach dropped out looking at the wound, it was sewn and cleaned, as if professionally done. With no idea what to do with it, Dan rewrapped it and took a few aspirin for the throbbing and tried not to think too hard about the loss. Jordan had taken one look at Dan's mangled hand and lost his fire for feuding.

Uncle Steve had fared a little better, and he was leaving the hospital as soon as someone came by to take out his IV, discharged with a mandate to rest and take his pain meds. He had gotten off light, the police told Jordan, with just a few scrapes and a bad bump on the back of his head. Dan wondered if this was due to the code Oliver had mentioned Finnoway having.

"Go to the police with what, exactly?" Dan asked. The overhead voices of nurses paging doctors broke in and out of their conversation. Dan tossed his waiting-room candy bar onto the chair next to him and sighed. "I guarantee you Finnoway is smart enough to have gotten rid of any evidence that I was in that funeral home. Unless he marches down the street waving my finger around, I think we're screwed."

He hadn't yet dropped the bomb that he needed to get his finger back from Finnoway, partly because the words stoppered up his throat with their insanity, and partly because it would only make their situation look more hopeless.

Abby regarded him silently from the bank of chairs directly across from him. Like all of them, she'd clearly spent the night sleeping in a hospital chair. Whatever. They only looked as crazy as they felt.

"We might not be able to prove anything, but going to the police would slow him down, at least," she finally said. Jordan leaned onto the chair behind her, tapping his foot. "And who knows, maybe there's a prior conviction we don't know about."

"He's running for city council, Abby. I'm betting all of his skeletons are hidden in better places than a closet," Dan said, shivering at the accidental choice of words.

"Well, we can't leave!" Jordan smacked his palms on the back of Abby's chair, startling her. "This is my home now, Dan. There's no way I'm going back to my parents." Jordan realized what he was saying and lowered his voice. "And we're not leaving here without you, either."

Dan knew this was meant to inspire him with confidence, but the sentiment only filled him with dread, reminding him just how trapped he was.

"What if we *can* find proof that Finnoway is the one who hurt you, or that he has ties to those criminals—"

"The Bone Artists," Dan supplied. His hand pulsed—ached—and he shuddered.

"Yes. What if we can prove it?" she asked

Dan avoided her imploring eyes, picking up his candy bar and fiddling with the torn wrapper. "This has been going on for years, Abby. Generations. If we get Finnoway tossed in jail, someone else will just show up to take his place."

"That's not a defeatist attitude or anything," Jordan muttered. "But it's the truth."

Stymied, they sat listening to the hospital pages and the nurse bantering with a drug-addled Steve in the nearby room. Oliver and Sabrina had suggested waiting, trying to bait Finnoway again, but this time together, with Dan in on it. He had no idea if he could trust them that far, or at all. That was the thing about someone lying to you—it was almost impossible to believe them ever again. Dan studied Abby and Jordan, wondering how they managed to have the friendship they did, even in spite of all the secrets and lies that had passed among them over the past twelve months. Seen in that light, maybe trusting Sabrina and Oliver made perfect sense.

More to the point, he didn't have the luxury of picking and choosing. He needed to move quickly.

"All right, we can try to gather some proof," Dan said softly, closing his eyes and squeezing them. "Where do we start?"

Chapter
35

*I*t wasn't exactly home, but after yesterday's ordeal, Dan felt incredibly lucky to be back in his little shared guest room in Uncle Steve's apartment. Steve was too doped up from the pain meds to notice the way Dan kept twisting away to conceal his right hand. Instead, he had camped out in the living room with the Xbox, snuggled up in a fuzzy robe and slippers. They had spent the previous night keeping an eye on him, fetching juice or food and generally making sure he was comfortable.

Early morning light crept across the carpet in wide squares. Abby and Jordan sat on the floor of the guest room, fresh notebooks opened to take dictation while Dan went through all the files Maisie Moore had given him. This time he didn't leave out the connection between Trax Corp. and Brookline, and it appalled his friends every bit as much as he'd known it would. At least he could take pride in the fact that this part of the Bone Artists' operations had already been shut down thanks to his parents' lifework.

But his parents had been better investigators than Dan and his friends were. The information in front of them was all so tangled up and circumstantial. He felt incredibly outnumbered, and worse, outwitted. He hated how much time this was taking, when meanwhile Finnoway was somewhere with his finger, no doubt already making plans to ruin him.

Dan squeezed his eyes shut. *You've gone awfully silent, Micah, when I could actually use your help. They took your body, didn't they? What do I do? How do I get it back?*

"What if we look into Finnoway's background? I'm convinced there's something there," Abby said. "We could go look on the computer in Uncle Steve's office. Or I could just pull him up on my phone."

"No!" Dan dropped down from the futon, almost batting her phone out of her hands. Instead, he awkwardly wrestled it from her with his left hand. "Don't you get it? They don't forgive and they don't forget. If you get caught poking around in his history it will just get worse, not better."

"God, I didn't even think of that," Jordan said, staring wide-eyed at both of them. "Not to sound incredibly selfish, but I really don't want a target on my back, either. Or my family's."

Dan stayed quiet, not pointing out that it was likely too late for that. He had no idea just how choosy the Bone Artists were. Uncle Steve had already been attacked once. Had he, Abby, and Jordan been added to their debt list of people to eradicate?

What if they went after his mom and dad? The parents who had taken him in after family after family had rejected him in the foster system? Dan couldn't let that happen. Paul and Sandy had been so good to him. They hadn't cared about his background. They'd treated him like a kid with a blank slate.

"That's the whole point," he said under his breath.

Abby tried to meet his eyes, but he dodged away from her, standing and turning to face the window.

"What's the whole point, Dan?"

"The Bone Artists are after *me* for what *my* birth parents did. You two aren't part of that, and you don't have to be. You can have a blank slate. Jordan is going to need that if he's going to keep living here." Dan felt like he had made this speech before, but he couldn't quite remember. God, which made him realize . . . He went to his bags and fished out his medication. At least the jerks hadn't stolen that, too.

He tossed back one of the pills, swallowing it dry. Then he stalked out of the room, heedless of how petulant it made him look. He stopped on the landing, hovering his right hand over the bannister while he tried and failed to outpace the thoughts fighting for supremacy in his head. His hand brushed the railing and his wound throbbed. He swore, snatching his hand back and holding it to his chest.

A single footstep creaked on the landing floor, and then the door to the guest room shut. He felt, rather than heard, Abby's presence at his back. Then her hand skimmed his shoulder and he couldn't help shivering. He felt cruelly, unaccountably *old*. And that wasn't fair, he reflected. He was still just a kid in so many ways. In most ways.

"Do you really think they would come after me and Jordan?"

Dan pulled in an unsteady breath. "Yes."

Her fingers tightened on his shoulder, and at last something other than fear cut to the forefront of his mind. He didn't want to give Abby up, not now, not next year. If anything, he wanted more of her.

"But you need our help, don't you?" she said.

"Honestly, I don't know." Dan sighed, and he felt her touch

recoil a fraction. "I appreciate that you're trying to stick by me in this, but I'm worried. . . . If something happens to you, either of you, I'll carry it with me for the rest of my life."

And that would finish me off. He felt strung together by a weak thread as it was, pushed well beyond exhausted and frayed.

"My parents were just trying to do the right thing," Dan added in a whisper. "And look what happened to them."

She leaned into him, gradually, hugging him from behind. He didn't dare move, afraid to startle her and ruin the moment. This was worth protecting, he thought, whatever that might mean in the end.

"Wouldn't it be nice if we could just put the whole damn thing on someone's else plate for a change?" he said.

Suddenly, her grasp around him tightened.

"Dan . . ." She pulled away, and reluctantly he turned to face her. "What if we could?"

"How? I mean, it's so far-fetched. . . . A respectable city councilman overseeing a gang of shadowy thugs? Who would buy it?" He hung his head, shaking it, then he leaned onto the bannister.

Abby grabbed his arm and squeezed it hard. "No, that doesn't matter. We don't have to say the incredible parts. We know where he works, yeah, but we saw those masked people go in the side door of his building. What if they're holding all the stolen bones in there? We can, I don't know, call in an anonymous tip to the police about a fire or a gunshot or something, anything just to get them *inside* and looking around. We don't have to go anywhere near Finnoway, and if it doesn't work, then there's no way to trace it back to us."

It wasn't the most elegant plan he had ever heard, but it was better than looking for proof in the files, which had amounted to nothing so far. He held her at arm's length, going over the idea again and again.

"Dan, if you really think he'll keep coming after you then I think the best way forward is to try and get him arrested. He has to be keeping the bones from the grave robberies somewhere, right?"

"And if there's nothing?" Dan asked. "Or if the police don't even go inside? What then?"

"Then we leave. Yes, even Jordan," she said in response to his unasked question. The desperation in her voice was definitely persuasive. "Finnoway never bothered you before you came to this city. Maybe he'll let it go."

Dan gave a watery laugh. "Abby, he didn't know I existed before. Why do you think my parents left me with Crawford as my last name? They didn't want me associated at all with the name Ash. Not that being a Crawford kept me out of harm's way."

It was too ironic not to laugh. His mother had tried to save him from being hunted, but it hadn't made a difference. Parents couldn't protect you from anything.

But he could protect Abby. He reached for her hand, finding it awkward to rely so much on his less-favored side.

"I don't know, Dan. I don't know what else to suggest."

"Abby, I'll try anything you think will work," he said honestly. "I'm just saying, if this doesn't work, you and Jordan need to leave it alone. You need to leave *me* alone. Finnoway's after me, and I won't let you two get caught in the middle."

"If only we had a contingency plan," Abby said, turning and leaning against the bannister. "*Someone* must be interested in everything we've found, even if the locals would never see past the councilman's charm and influence. I wonder. . . ."

She stopped, and Dan watched her mouth move silently as she worked something out. "If we plant the idea that Maisie Moore's death wasn't an accident, then maybe we can get *someone* to care," she said. "Like her fellow journalists at the *Metairie Daily*."

Dan followed, almost tripping on his words with eagerness. "Fellow journalists whose job it is to see connections like these."

"Coworkers," Abby finished, "who would be interested in the truth." He wanted to pick her up and squeeze her, but she was already racing down the hall and back to the guest room. "I'll make the phone call!"

That was when the knock came at the front door.

Chapter 36

*T*here are certain kinds of knocks, and Dan knew the one at Uncle Steve's front door was not the happy kind. A fist rattled once, twice, and then a voice drifted through the open foyer and up the stairs.

"NOPD, open up."

"Probably just here to follow up about the break-in," Abby said lightly, jogging down the stairs to get the door. Dan could still hear Uncle Steve playing the Xbox in the downstairs living room.

Jordan emerged onto the landing, pulling on a sweatshirt. "What's the noise?"

"Police are here," Abby called over her shoulder as she reached the door. "Maybe they found your laptop. Fingers crossed, hm?"

"Don't open it." Dan reached for the bannister with his good hand, clutching it. "Just . . . don't."

His stomach roiled, empty except for a few bites of candy bar, but feeling ill didn't preclude the fact that he felt *wrong*.

"It's the police, Dan, I have to answer it," she said, frowning. She was already turning the knob, and Dan knew instinctively to brace.

The cop behind the door shouldered it open the rest of the

275

way, knocking into Abby. He mumbled a noncommittal apology while she stumbled back.

"Excuse me," she murmured, grabbing the wall for balance. "Can we help you, officer? Are you here about the break-in?"

"Yes," he said coldly, his eyes sweeping the foyer and then up the stairs. When he noticed Dan, a shallow smile pricked at his lips. "Yes, I am. You Daniel Crawford?"

The hairs on the back of Dan's neck stood on end. So Oliver was right. The blood, his fingerprint, his DNA . . . He had gotten away from Finnoway once, but now Finnoway was going to make sure that it never happened again. Dan glanced over his shoulder, but the only way out besides the front door was a rickety old fire escape and then a seven-foot drop to the ground. And if he ran, he would be resisting arrest; he had no idea what that would allow the cop to do to him.

Wouldn't that just be the perfect, tidy ending that Finnoway probably wanted?

"I'm Dan Crawford," he said, going numb. He turned and marched robotically down the stairs. Cooperation seemed like his only option. There had to be some way to CSI himself out of this; if his blood had been planted somewhere, couldn't they tell it was squirted out of a syringe or whatever?

"Thanks for making this easy," the officer continued. He was tall and broad, not at all the stereotype of a doughy, out-of-shape cop. His close-cropped red hair was beginning to curl out around the edges of his cap. The little nametag on his jacket read *Conlen James*.

"It's always better when you make it easy." The officer gestured for Dan to hurry it up.

"What the hell? What are you doing?" Jordan shouted, racing to the top of the stairs. "What are the charges? You can't just take him."

"Daniel Crawford, you're under arrest for the murder of Tamsin Pelicie. You have the right to remain silent. Anything you say can and will be used against you in a court of law." Officer James ran through the speech, but Dan wasn't listening. His entire body had gone cold at the start of it, no sound penetrating his skull for an entire minute. He was drifting, falling.

Murder? Him? It wasn't possible. . . . Even Finnoway wouldn't try to pin something so heinous on him.

But it would lock you away forever. Of course he would.

"Murder?" Abby shrieked, breathless. She crowded the door, trying to slow down the officer, but he pushed her aside easily. "How? He's been with us all this time! He has an alibi!"

Dan crumpled. She was wrong. There *was* a gap of time that nobody but he could account for. Even Oliver and Sabrina didn't know how he had ended up at their store. For the whole stretch of morning after which he had suspiciously left his friends at the hospital, he had no alibi whatsoever.

"That's not what the evidence says."

"That was fast," Dan bit out sarcastically, but he didn't pause as he walked toward the door. "It's blood, isn't it? My blood? Doesn't it usually take some time to process blood at a crime scene?"

CSI, don't fail me now.

"Not always," Officer James said through clenched teeth. He grabbed Dan by the shoulder and spun him around,

guiding him roughly toward the door. "See, we take murder real serious in this town."

"As a crime or a hobby?" It was a stupid thing to say, but the officer simply snorted and prodded his shoulder, hard, letting his knuckle dig in. "I wouldn't get cute if I were you."

Jordan followed close on their heels, drawing a grimace from the officer. Both of his friends stayed right with Dan as he was maneuvered out the door and down the stairs.

"Where are you taking him?" Jordan demanded. "Dan, I'll talk to Uncle Steve, we'll get you a lawyer. We'll figure something out!"

Both of his friends were frantic now, trying to crane their heads over the officer's shoulder to see Dan. The police car was parked half on the curb, its lights spinning silently, bathing the building in flashes of red and blue.

"I hope your little friends don't interfere," the officer was saying. "Wouldn't want to have to bring them in, too."

Tears gathered in his eyes, itchy and hot. This was too soon. He needed more time. There had to be a way out of this, a way to prove his innocence.

He was so overwhelmed, it didn't even faze him that the black motorcycle was there, its rider clad in midnight leathers, watching from behind the helmet. It would almost be weirder if the motorcyclist *wasn't* there, since he or she was undoubtedly one of Finnoway's little minions, watching and keeping tabs. Dan gave a bitter smile.

"Take a picture," he said. "It will last longer."

The fear, late in coming, slammed into him then. If only there was video, maybe some kind of security footage, that would exonerate him. But Finnoway would be careful to destroy that, too. *If, if, if.* He struggled, trying to shake off the policeman's cruel grip on his arm. "Can't you just take a swab or something? Isn't that enough? I'll volunteer it."

Which was stupid, he knew. He should ask to see a warrant, fight this, do something. . . .

They have my bones.

"Or a fingerprint! Can't I do that here somehow?" His voice climbed into a terrified-little-boy register, the words cracking open with panic.

"Nope."

Officer James opened the door of the car to let him in. Stale, human smells wafted out from the back, cigarettes and urine and sweat. Dan felt a strong hand on his head, forcing him to duck. It was like a dungeon, he knew, one he would never escape. His only hope was that someone at the station would listen, but who would believe his crazy story?

"Don't say anything, Dan! Just keep quiet! We'll do something! We'll get you help!" Jordan was screaming. He ran up to the window just after the door was slammed shut. The officer didn't seem to care that his friends were scrabbling at the window, waving, tapping, just trying to make one last little connection through the glass.

"I'll make the call!" Abby shouted, pounding on the window. "I'll make it!"

Dan stared at them, trembling, his hands frozen at his sides. His voice would sound muffled to them, he knew, when he spoke the single sentence from inside: "Tell Oliver they have me."

Chapter
37

*D*an had never been arrested before. The last time he had been questioned by the police, he had at least had the benefit of his parents there beside him. Now he was alone, waiting in a tiny shoe box of a room with patched walls. It was almost hilarious how perfectly *policey* it was, with the two-way mirror and spare, metal table. The air conditioning was kicked up so high he could feel the cold of the chair through his jeans.

He wondered if Finnoway was on the other side of that mirrored glass. Was his reach that far? Or was it enough simply to fake a break-in and plant Dan's DNA on a piece of broken glass or a spot of carpet? Ingenious, really; once they had part of his body, they had *him*.

He thought of Abby and Jordan back at the apartment, panicking, trying in vain to help him out of a situation that had no happy ending. He should have told them about Oliver's suspicions, that his finger wouldn't be used for twisted old magics, but for sabotage. But what could his friends truly *do*? If anything, Oliver and his rifle seemed like a better bet.

The police had confiscated his phone and wallet, leaving him utterly without connection to the outside world or his identity. He would get a phone call soon and eventually a lawyer, but somehow he didn't think that lawyer would be very sympathetic to his story.

No, if it came to a trial, he had the horrible feeling already that he would be put in prison for murder.

The lights in the shoe-box room abruptly cut out. Dan shivered in the piercing cold, looking up and around, trying to make sense of the shadows that pressed in on every side. It was torture. They weren't even going to treat him like a human being.

His wound was bothering him, the aspirin having long since worn off.

The door to the room opened and closed in one breath, the flash of outside light cutting in so quickly he didn't have a chance to turn and see who had entered the room before he was shuttered into complete darkness again.

A rush of cold brought every hair on his body to attention, and then a face emerged across the table, growing out of the darkness like a pale and deathly flower. He had never noticed how much Finnoway's head, with its sparse hair, square jaw, and high cheekbones, resembled a skull.

"You," Dan said weakly.

"In the flesh." Finnoway smiled at him, breezy, the lights sputtering back on, but only lighting the room enough for Dan to see to the ends of his hands. "Speaking of, I hear you're missing a bit of that."

"Thanks to you."

Finnoway sat on the edge of the rectangular metal table. His suit was black, making him melt into the edges of the murky darkness. He had tucked a briefcase under one arm. Clucking his tongue, he wagged a finger at Dan.

"Now, now, careful with those baseless accusations, son."

"Don't call me that," Dan growled.

"But that's what you are," Finnoway said casually, opening the briefcase and balancing it on one thigh. "You are whatever I say you are. You are *whoever* I say you are. My son, my nephew, my paper boy . . ." He tossed a single piece of paper onto the table and it spun out toward Dan, landing upside down. Dan reached for it, twisting the edges so he could read the print. A birth certificate. His.

"Where did you get this?" he stammered, yanking his hands back as if scalded.

"This is going to be a real education for you." Finnoway rummaged in the briefcase again, this time bringing out a stack of photographs. He laid them out one at a time on the table. "There's a bin under the table if you need it."

Dan soon understood why. The photos, playing out in chronological order, made his stomach clench in horror.

"Micah was a good boy. A *loyal* boy. Oliver tries to be, but he's a predictable failure, given his idiot family. You know, when Oliver turned you in, I thought you were just a stroke of luck. Here comes Danny Ash," he said playfully, almost giggling, "the last little loose end to be snipped. But it's worse than all that, isn't it? Micah was one of us, and you watched him die. You did nothing while he was *murdered*."

Dan's throat felt like sandpaper. He couldn't speak or tear his eyes away from the pictures being lined up in front of him.

"And now you've gone and murdered my assistant, Daniel. That was very bad of you." Finnoway's smile endured, as did his singsong tone. "You see, here is where you wrestled her to the ground. Tamsin was strong, but you're stronger, aren't you? And this one is where you punched out a few of her teeth. When

that didn't satisfy you, the pliers did. There are a lot of teeth in the human mouth, more than you might expect. It takes a long, long, *agonizingly* long time to pluck out all thirty-two."

Dan shook and finally turned away. The last picture was too much, just a gaping, empty mouth. He could feel that tiny bit of hospital candy bar rolling around nauseatingly in his stomach. Her smile had been pretty and perfect, and now there was nothing left of it at all.

A soft rustling drew Dan's attention, even if he refused to look at the horrifying photos. Finnoway produced a small black velvet bag and upturned it. A cascade of glittering white teeth spilled onto the table, scattering and rolling, dropping off the table and twinkling like falling beads.

"She fought back, though, didn't she? The spitfire . . . Going so far as to bite off your little finger."

Finnoway's grin was slow and easy, and the way he deliberately emphasized each word made Dan cling to the chair under him. It wasn't possible, was it? But he hadn't seen the raw wound of his taken finger. He had no idea how it had been done, or with what. . . .

He doubled over, reaching for the bucket and retching up the contents of his stomach.

"You can get a person to do anything, provided the right motivation is given," Finnoway added softly, flicking away one of the fallen teeth that had landed too close to his expensive trousers.

Dan wiped at the sour taste in his mouth, relieved when Finnoway gathered up the photos like a spread of playing cards and tucked them back into the briefcase. "S-so what do you want me to do?" Dan croaked. "What's my motivation?"

"I want you to rot in prison for the rest of your meaning-less life, because you're an *Ash*, and just like your mother, you can't seem to help but get annoyingly underfoot," Finnoway told him with a faraway smile. "And you will. Rot in prison, I mean. You take medication, don't you? Mild dissociative disorder? You lose time occasionally, right? Minutes, even hours . . . Plenty of time to murder an innocent girl and flee the scene."

Dan shook his head fiercely. No, no, this wasn't right. It couldn't happen this easily. He couldn't be this powerless. "I haven't had an episode in a long time."

"Are you sure?"

Dan thought back to the night in the Ninth Ward, when he'd lost so much time on the way home and had to recall it in pieces. He remembered falling asleep in the taxicab this morning, and wondering how it could have happened so fast. Those hadn't been blackouts, surely?

"You see," Finnoway said smartly. "You've had them—your whole life, you've had them. And that's all a jury will need to hear about that. Your little finger lodged in a dead girl's throat will just be the icing on top."

Dan felt boneless. Defeated. He sat back heavily against the chair, pinned there by the waves of nausea and terror that seemed to crash over him one after another. He knew the ques-tion he wanted to ask, and so he did it, even though it hardly mattered now. He would be branded a murderer—in all the history books, the files, the photos, this would be his legacy. His life.

"You killed my parents," he said softly. Sadly.

"They took a long dive off a steep cliff in a Cadillac," the Artificer replied with a shrug. "That's not something most survive."

"But *you* did it," Dan whispered, tremulous with rage. If he didn't keep control he would lash out, dive across the table and throttle Finnoway just like Finnoway claimed Dan had throttled Tamsin. He might as well earn his sentence. "You drove them to it."

"And you would never be able to prove as much."

It was tempting to play his hand, to tell Finnoway about the call Abby was making to Maisie's coworkers in hopes that it would buy him some leverage. But that would be a mistake. He didn't want Finnoway on their trail at all. He needed time. Time for Abby and Jordan to get help before one of Finnoway's people got to them first.

Dan looked at the teeth scattered across the table and closed his eyes. He did have one bit of leverage left. One desperate hope to trade up. "What's worth more to you, me sitting in jail or a powerful talisman? A person's blood means something to you people, right? Their legacy determines the talisman? Luck turns into luck, power turns into power. That is, if those things even work."

"Of course they work," Finnoway sneered, squinting down his beak of a nose at Dan. "What do you know about it?"

"I don't know anything about it," Dan lied. "But I know my family tree. And my family tree doesn't just have Ashes, it has Crawfords. Go ahead, look it up. Look up Warden Daniel Crawford. The man did all kinds of experiments. He knew a lot about passing on a legacy. I bet his bones would make a mean talisman. I could tell you where they are."

"This is an amusing game, but I'm not interested in playing."

Dan shrugged, hoping he looked more confident than he felt. His stomach trembled, threatening another vomiting spell. "Your loss."

The Artificer circled him, watching, buzzard-like and silent. Then he paused behind Daniel's chair, and in the dim light of the room, Dan could see the glow of a mobile phone reflecting off the metal table. Finnoway was reading.

"Hm." A chilly pause. "Interesting. More interesting than an Ash, that's for certain."

"So what does that mean?" Dan asked. "Still want me to rot in prison?"

Finnoway's dark laugh echoed off the walls and in his head. "Oh, you'll still rot, Daniel, but now that I know how powerful your blood is, you'll be rotting in pieces."

Chapter

38

"*D*oes your wife know you're a complete head case?" Dan asked, swaying slightly in the passenger seat of Finnoway's car.

He had been handcuffed, and with the help of Officer James—who it turned out wouldn't have required much evidence at all to bring Dan in—smuggled out down a long, narrow hallway and through the back door of the police station. They had hurried him across the parking lot, perhaps nervous about drawing attention. That gave Dan hope, at least. He was tempted to scream to try to get help right then, but Officer James had a gun, and there was also the matter of Finnoway's two new assistants, who were waiting to meet them. They were both young women, dressed as sharply and cleanly as Tamsin once was, but Dan could see a bulge under each of their blazers. Three armed captors would be hard to escape.

Now those two armed women sat in the back of the black Rolls-Royce, silently keeping an eye on Dan and Finnoway in the front. But Dan was interested in the wedding band on Finnoway's hand. He was trying to imagine the woman who would marry him.

Finnoway rested one wrist lazily on the steering wheel as he drove, and laughed wryly at Dan's question. His cufflinks flashed in the afternoon sunlight—tiny silver molars. "I'm surprised at you, Dan. I thought your generation was supposed to be so progressive. Do you think that just because she's a woman and a mother she's some kind of blameless saint?"

"She married you," Dan replied darkly. "So I guess that means she's a total nightmare, too."

"If pressed, I'd say Briony is the more sadistic of the two of us," Finnoway answered. It was a serene observation, one he made with a fond, distant smile. Ugh. Dan didn't want to know what kind of moment he was remembering. "Sorry to say you probably won't be making her acquaintance. She's rarely at the Catacomb at this time of day. Little Jessy has Tae Kwon Do."

Jesus. They made the Bender family look like the Brady Bunch.

"She doesn't ride motocross, does she?" Dan asked bitterly. It would be just so fitting if his shadow on a motorcycle was Finnoway's batshit wife.

"Not to my knowledge. Why?"

Dan huddled against the window, weak with hunger and a more insistent, gnawing feeling that left him feeling sore and fragile. "No reason."

His hand ached, but he didn't want to give Finnoway the satisfaction of seeing him in pain. Dan clenched his jaw, trying to ignore the persistent throb and burn.

The route from the police station gradually turned familiar—Dan had gone up and down these same streets twice now, once when chasing the masked vandals, and again when he traced his way back to the funerary home. He didn't need to be told where to walk, though the Artificer's assistants helped him along anyway. They were headed to the basement door, Dan knew. He noticed they were shuffling over a deep, single tire tread in the pavement as they marched him up to the curb.

The main, silver door of the first floor was X-ed with police tape that fluttered over the open space. This must have been where Finnoway had set up the supposed crime scene. Dan flinched and turned away, remembering those horrible photos. He didn't bother to hope that Finnoway had made things painless for Tamsin. He didn't want to know how it all had really happened. Finnoway's version of events was the only one that really mattered now anyway.

Dan's hand throbbed as if in sympathy; he was not looking forward to the day when he removed the bandage and had to look at the damage on a regular basis.

Please, God, when I look closer don't let there be teeth marks.

Just before he was shuffled through the door, Dan saw the familiar black motorcycle parked a little ways down the block, just beyond the police tape. Behind it, the back of the office building across the street had been heavily graffitied with the same white chalky paint he'd found outside Steve's apartment. Instead of the French sentence he remembered, though, this mark had symbols he didn't recognize.

"What do they mean?" he asked idly. Finnoway didn't seem interested in holding anything back now that he had Dan trapped in every possible sense.

Finnoway's glitzy watch flashed as he flicked his hand at a circular symbol with a slash running through it. "That one means we're low on toilet paper."

"What? Really?" Dan stumbled a little over the uneven ground. Then they were inside the door, and he slowed down, trying to stall.

"No, not really. Keep walking, you're boring me."

Instead of heading in the direction Dan had gone last time, Finnoway took them left at the corridor. They passed through a series of nondescript rooms before finally stopping outside a heavy, ancient-looking door under an arched doorway. Finnoway rapped three times on this door, and then Dan heard a key turning from the inside, scraping the metal noisily before the creak of locks and hinges gave and the door stuttered open. A breath of musty sewer air flooded out to meet them, wet and choking.

"Never heard of Febreze, I take it?" Dan was shoved unceremoniously through the archway and into a cool, dank hall. A figure in a dog mask was there to greet them, and it was impossible to tell through the mask whether the person was surprised to see Dan or not.

"I'm glad you've turned the corner on sullen," Finnoway said, shouldering up next to Dan. He was taller, however, and had to duck his head to safely navigate the tunnel. "But you won't rile me up, Daniel, though your attempts do hint at a joie de vivre I wouldn't have counted on from you. Your parents were pathetically easy to wipe out. I'm glad you're interested in making things more fun."

The door slammed shut behind them, leaving them in momentary blackness. Dan's vision adjusted, showing an ordinary brick tunnel. There was nothing particularly sinister about it, though Finnoway's presence at his side kept him in a constant state of alert unease.

Finally, the passage around them widened. Still, Dan pulled his shoulders in close to his body, finding that they were watched on both sides by Bone Artists in their crude, crumpled animal masks.

"Why do they wear those things?" Dan asked, averting his eyes from the watchers, their heads turning slightly to follow his progress.

"Mardi Gras was always the easiest time of year to do our work," Finnoway explained sternly. "The tradition kept."

On and on they went, the air turning more tepid and rank while also getting cooler, the smell of wet mud and worms tickling his nose. He had no idea how Finnoway could navigate in such total darkness, but the man's grip on him was sure, and Dan began to get the hang of measuring each step before taking the next.

At last, they reached the end of the tunnel, where they were greeted by another door. It was illuminated on either side by torches that flickered over uneven, craggy walls. Dan wished the torches would go out. In this newfound light, he could see that surrounding them, cemented into the ceiling and walls, were hundreds upon hundreds of white, grinning skulls.

Chapter
39

It was just the two of them in the corridor of bones, but still Dan didn't struggle. Where would he go? He would trip and flail back through the tunnel behind them, only to meet thirty or so assailants hungry to fall on him.

Dan never should have mentioned the warden to Finnoway. He would gladly take his chances in court, or even a lifetime in prison, over this. How many times did he have to learn that things could always get worse?

His steps slowed. Everything felt hopeless. Just putting one foot in front of the next felt like too much to ask.

"You're weak. We'll get you some food and water," Finnoway said, pushing Dan farther down the corridor.

"I don't want anything from you."

"You'll eat what you're given."

Dan shook his head, leaning forward into his heavy steps. "I know what happens to people who eat food in the underworld. They can't leave."

Finnoway smiled darkly. "I was still thinking about Hansel and Gretel, but that's good. I'll use that."

On the other side of the door, they came into a huge, vaulted space with floodlights and scaffolding. The tunnel must have connected them to another building. It reminded Dan of an

archeological dig, with shelves balanced against the outer walls and crates littering the floor and some of the scaffolding flats. Straw stuck out of some of the crates and packing peanuts spilled out of others. Dan smelled and tasted gritty dust on the air.

An enormous fabric flag hung from the center of the ceiling, aged white with black paint lettering across it.

THESE WERE THE RULES AS THEY WERE FIRST
PUT DOWN:
First, that the Artist should choose an Object dear to the
deceased.
Second, that the Artist feel neither guilt nor remorse in
the taking.
Third, and most important, that the Object would not
hold power until blooded. And that the more innocent the
blood for the blooding, the more powerful the result.

Dan wondered if that was an actual code of conduct or just more legendary nonsense to keep the populace afraid of the mere *possibility* of the Bone Artists existing. But they were beyond possibility now, and judging by the number of skulls Dan had seen on the way in, these people were not about idle threats.

The shelves along the walls were overflowing with deep plastic buckets, each one marked with a name in huge, black block letters. Dan scanned the names. Most of them were unfamiliar, but others he recognized.

CRAWFORD, M.

BERKLEY, E.

BERKLEY, R.

BONHEUR, M.

He couldn't take his eyes away from the box marked with his father's name. His body felt hollowed out, all of his will and fight gone.

A bin labeled *BERKLEY, O.* was still on the ground, open and empty. It occurred to him that he should warn Oliver that they were coming for him next, but that was ridiculous. He'd never leave there alive.

And now Dan would have a bin of his own, and parts of him would be transformed and sold, and his doomed bloodlines could make life miserable for someone else.

Maybe he could warn Oliver as a ghost, the way Micah had tried to warn him.

He wasn't a ghost yet, his hand reminded him helpfully, stinging beneath the bandages. A dozen or so Bone Artists were here, too, wandering the vault, their masks removed and clipped to their waistbands or belts. There was no uniformity among them that Dan could detect. Some were young, some were old, all races and genders represented.

"Get him something to eat," Finnoway was saying, snapping his fingers at a man who nodded and scampered down an adjoining hall. A few low archways went off in different directions, but there was no telling where they led.

"So is this where you make the talismans, or just where you organize everything to ship?" Dan asked, casting his eyes around the huge expanse of the vault. Finnoway didn't try to stop him from wandering around the outer wall. He looked almost pleased, noting the impressed look on Dan's face.

"I'd rather not give you a lengthy explanation of the process," he replied. "It would be a waste of breath, considering how soon you'll be dead."

Dan gulped.

"What if I had something more valuable for you? Something I could offer."

"That doesn't work twice," Finnoway said. "You already traded up. The trick somewhat loses its effect the more you do it."

Dan stopped at one of the messy tables, on which several cardboard boxes sat open, revealing alphabetized labels. Inside the boxes were hundreds upon hundreds of folders, not unlike the ones Dan had found back in the funeral home. In fact, these might have been the same folders, transported in stacks—Dan could see what looked like the Ash folder now; it was right on top with its silly pen doodle on the cover.

With the feeling that he had nothing much to lose, Dan lifted the folder with his left hand and opened it.

Chapter 40

*I*mmediately, he heard the echoing clap of Finnoway's shoes behind him, but the man made no move to restrain or interrupt.

The folder had a lot more in it besides the funeral arrangements Dan had found inside earlier. There were notes and maps, and Dan found copies of the articles Maisie Moore had given him. There was even a transcript of testimony from what sounded like the trial that ultimately shut down Trax Corp., in 1995. The closing statement for the defense read:

> These accusations are absurd. Trax Corp. and Jacob Finnoway are blameless.
> These are just the mad rantings of an environmental fanatic, a fanatic who is
> currently evading arrest for trespassing and so refuses even to appear before
> us to testify. There is simply no hard, compelling evidence that this "under
> the table" drug ring ever existed. All we have are these conspiracy reports
> from a journalist who won't even reveal her sources.

There was something strange about the statement, but Dan couldn't quite put his finger on what it was. Something in the back of his brain wasn't lining up. "Who's Jacob? An alias of yours?"

"My brother," Finnoway replied casually. "Your witch of a mother ruined his life."

Dan let the papers fall out of his hands, not caring that they landed in jumbled disarray. Dozens and dozens of photos had been taken of his parents, all obviously from a distance, taken with a telephoto spying lens when they weren't aware of it.

"Wish I could say I was sorry."

His mother had stumbled onto the connection between Trax Corp. and Brookline, even if she'd been many years too late to stop the warden's experiments. If only she'd known that Trax Corp. itself was a front, she might still be alive. Of course, he thought darkly, Dan had gone digging around in all the history, too, and even though he was paying the price for not learning from his mistakes, it was a comfort to know there was a part of his legacy he was *proud* of. The part that cared about uncovering the truth.

"Something funny?" Finnoway asked, leaning closer.

"You wouldn't get it," Dan murmured. He studied the Artificer. Finnoway looked so absolutely assured of his victory, it only made Dan want that much more to find some way to outsmart him.

Sighing, defeated, Dan turned back to the folder. He held up a photo of his parents huddling under an umbrella. The city behind them was a blur of gray and brown. It was impossible to tell the location, but their faces were in focus. Evelyn leaned into his father, her head tucked under his chin. Finnoway had started yapping again, chatting to the Bone Artist who had returned with food, but Dan wasn't paying attention. He was distracted by a tiny, bright crest on his mother's jacket, red and white, a minuscule beacon.

DUCATI.

His heart leapt to his throat. He hustled back to the other side of the vault, ignoring the sandwich and soda that had been

laid out for him on a small card table at the center of the room. Finnoway watched him with crossed arms, grinning a little as Dan breezed by, accurately guessing where Dan was headed.

"Would you like me to get it down? You can say good-bye to your father in person."

Dan did his best to ignore the sting of that barb. "My father . . . Just my father. Why isn't there a bucket for my mother?"

That cool, charming smile of Finnoway's faltered. It was quick and he tried to catch himself, but Dan saw it. Finnoway uncrossed his arms and stuck his hands in his pockets. "Their car crashed into a river. Her body was washed away."

"So you don't have it," Dan needled, returning to the card table. He took a seat on the stool provided and forced himself to take a bite of the sandwich. There might be a moment soon when he would need his strength. Chewing, swallowing, cracking open the soda, he crossed one leg over the other and played his one and only card.

"You don't have a bucket for my mother," he said firmly, "because she's still alive."

Chapter

41

*D*an waited for Finnoway's incredulous laughter to subside before adding softly, "I want to trade up. Again."

"With what? What could you possibly have that I would want?"

The Bone Artists milling about the vault gradually stopped what they were doing and turned their attention to Finnoway and Dan. One set down a tiny drill, dusting bone grit from his gloved hands before turning to listen.

Dan took another bite of the sandwich and washed it down with soda. "She's still alive," he repeated, "and I know where to find her."

He'd realized what was off about the trial testimony. Maisie Moore had told him that his parents had died a mere week after Trax Corp. got shut down in the trial. It was the same year the *Whistle* folded, 1995. But Dan hadn't been born until '96.

And that motorcycle. The Ducati jacket. The person stalking them across the country hadn't been taking pictures for Finnoway. It was Evie, and he knew it now. But there was no way to prove to Finnoway that he'd seen her. And if he could—if he played this card and traded his debt in for hers—it meant his mother, who had evaded the Bone Artists for so many years, might finally be caught.

He had to risk it. She'd abandoned him all those years ago. Really, he was repaying two debts in one. He hesitated to use the word *deserve* in this case, but maybe she really did deserve some kind of comeuppance for leaving him to whatever foster-family fate awaited him. Sure, he had gotten lucky with Sandy and Paul, but only after years of being made to feel like he wasn't wanted. And if Paul and Sandy hadn't taken him in, well—she might have doomed him to a much harder, lonelier life. Anyway, she seemed capable of taking care of herself. Finnoway might not actually best her, given her talent for evasion.

For leaving.

"She's been following me and my friends for days. I've seen her at least four times now. Today, even."

That wiped the smile off Finnoway's face for good. He took three menacing steps toward Dan, lording over him with his height and his cold, chiseled face. "How is this a bargain?"

Swallowing proved a challenge, especially because Dan hated the next thing he had to say. He would take his chances, and now so would she. "If I show you where to find her, you'll agree to stop hunting me. You'll get me out of this bogus murder charge, and you'll leave my friends alone, too."

He could see the Artificer weighing his options, chewing the inside of his mouth as his bright green eyes searched Dan's face for the truth.

"You're bluffing," Finnoway finally said.

"If she was dead, you would have her here," Dan replied. "She's been trying to reach out to me. I just didn't realize it until now."

The room went frigid. Nobody moved or spoke, and Dan's hand burned with pain. He could hear the faint *drip-drip* of a distant faucet counting out the seconds as Finnoway made up his mind.

"Where is she?"

Dan finished the sandwich, taking an unsteady breath. He had bet correctly—his mother was a bigger prize than the warden's blood. Sure, Dan was related to her, but he hadn't ruined the family business or Jacob Finnoway's life, and apparently the strength of the grudge overrode his valuable DNA.

"You'll tell me right now!" Finnoway bellowed it in Dan's face, the façade cracking for an instant before Finnoway collected himself, leaning back and tugging on his tie. "All right, Daniel, we're bargaining. So bargain."

Time. He had bought himself time. He wasn't so sure about the cost, but he could worry more about that later. If he lived.

He didn't know if he was trusting Oliver, his friends, or his theoretically still-living mother to save him. But he was desperate here, and his odds aboveground were better than they were down here. He *did* trust Abby's plan. If nothing else, even if he didn't survive, a new crop of journalists would rise to try to take the Bone Artists down.

"Take me back up. I want to see my friends and tell them I'm okay, then I'll bring you to her. You don't have to take the cuffs off. I won't run."

Finnoway snarled down into his face. "Maybe I underestimated you. You'd sell out your own mother?"

Dan nodded, slowly, fighting a tremor in his chin. "She left

me. All this time she was gone, I didn't know if she was dead or just didn't want me. But now it doesn't matter. I choose my new parents and I choose my friends. I choose the family I made. I choose me."

Chapter 42

$\mathcal{D}$an had never been so relieved to see sunlight in his life.

There it was, just a few slivers of it peeking from beneath the final door to freedom, and it filled him with hope. Even if he survived, there was the minor, itsy-bitsy matter of him facing a murder charge with evidence stacked against him.

But for now, he was alive. And after everything, he trusted deep down that his friends wouldn't abandon him to his fate.

The alley, smelly and damp, was a welcome reprieve after the stifling air of the Bone Artists' Catacomb. Dan glanced down toward Rampart Street, seeing Finnoway's Rolls-Royce there, already running and waiting for them. He glanced desperately in the other direction, but the motorcycle was no longer there. Onto the next phase in his last-ditch improvisation.

The two assistants were at the car, ready to intercept Dan from Finnoway, preventing any chance of him running.

"If you're lying," Finnoway whispered in his ear, clinging hard to his back, "I will keep you awake as I remove your bones one at a time, starting with the rest of your fingers."

Dan flinched.

Finnoway chuckled and wrangled Dan toward the backseat of the car. "Maybe I'll let Briony handle it."

The car blocked off the entrance to the alley, and if Dan didn't duck inside soon, the assistants would probably cram him in using force. He didn't think those ladies would hesitate to use the weapons he saw outlined beneath their blazers. He scanned the sidewalk on the other side of the car, peering into the coffee shop he'd seen the other night, hoping someone, anyone, would see him and notice something odd was going on.

Come on, please. . . . Someone please be there.

But there was nobody. He went limp, scrambling to think of how he was going to get out of this.

"Dan!"

His heart stopped, his heels skidding out on the pavement. He whipped his head up to see Abby and Jordan sprinting toward the Rolls-Royce from across the street. A horn blasted, and both of them stumbled back, narrowly avoiding the front bumper of a truck that sped down the road. Dan felt Finnoway's grip give on his cuffs and then felt a hard, round barrel poking into his lower back.

"Tell them to turn around and leave, or I'll shoot. It's silenced, and your body will be in the car and driven away before anyone's the wiser," Finnoway warned, one hand on Dan's left shoulder, the other digging the gun into his back.

Dan opened his mouth to shout to his friends, but a pop and a crack rent the air, loud enough to echo above the noises of the city. A bullet buried its way into the bricks of the building immediately to their left. Dan tried to follow the sound, dragging his eyes up from Jordan and Abby to the roof above the café. A young man's silhouette blazed against the wan afternoon clouds. Oliver and his rifle. So he was intent on making good on his promise. His friends had all come for him.

Dan couldn't see Sabrina, but he had a feeling she was somewhere else, maybe hidden, and hopefully armed with more than the baseball bat.

We're all going to jail, he thought wildly, excitedly, imagining the police cars that would arrive any second to respond to the gunshot. The funeral home was already on their radar from the supposed break-in. Dan tossed his head, trying to signal Oliver to stop before Finnoway ended him.

"Just turn around!" he shouted to his friends, going still when he heard Finnoway cock the gun pressed to his back. "Don't come any closer! Tell Oliver to stop firing!"

A crowd began to gather in the coffee shop across the street. Dan could see the scared faces pressing up to the window, a few customers on their cell phones or holding on to one another.

Jordan and Abby hesitated in the middle of the street, then seemed to sense Dan's urgency and carefully backed up to the sidewalk. There was just a road separating them, but they couldn't have felt farther away. Dan froze, helpless. If the police didn't get here *now*, he wasn't sure how he could get them all out of this alive.

If any of them was going to die, though, it should be *him*. He'd meant what he said to Finnoway in the Catacomb. Jordan and Abby really felt like family to him, only deeper because they were the family he'd chosen. And if he died now, all those faces in the coffee-shop window would see Finnoway lose his temper, and it would be too big, too messy to cover up.

"Get in the car," Finnoway roared, stabbing the gun harder into Dan's lower back.

He moved inch by inch, watching a shadow appear next to Oliver on the roof, then take form. Even from his spot on the ground, Dan could make out the rough, terrible shape of the person's rabbit mask.

"No!" Dan shouted. "Oliver!" He spun to face Finnoway as best he could. "You said nobody would get hurt! I told you to leave my friends alone."

A visible sweat had broken out on the Artificer's face, his calm demeanor shattered. He let out a hoarse laugh and prodded Dan again. "I lied."

Chapter
43

*D*an had never watched someone fall like that—slow at first but then all at once, picking up speed and barreling to the ground so fast there was almost no time to blink between fall and impact.

Someone screamed, a woman, and Dan lost sensation in his arms and back. He knew the gun was there, ready to fire, and he knew Oliver had just tumbled three stories to the pavement. He heard the cry and the dry crunch of Oliver's body meeting the ground, but nothing else seemed real or important in that moment.

He threw his weight against Finnoway, hard, ducking down and smashing his head into the man's sternum. Something cracked under his skull, not his bones but Finnoway's, and he heard the *click-clack* of the gun skimming across the paving stones. Someone was shouting again, screaming, and he felt Finnoway's sweat slide across his skin as he pushed and pushed.

Pain exploded in his back, again and again. But the feeling was gone, and he shrugged off the hurt, rearing up and throwing himself at the Artificer again. He was blind, crazed, but maybe that was what he needed now.

Dan tumbled with Finnoway, first onto the hood of the car, then into the street. The blows at his back stopped, but now

he could feel the aches creeping in. He was on his knees, half-tangled with Finnoway, who scrabbled onto his back, trying to push Dan off. Dan didn't feel strong, but he felt desperate, and the constant screaming and blood rushing in his ears only fortified that feeling. He tried to crush Finnoway down into the pavement. There was no plan anymore, no reason, just a terrible urge to watch this bastard's skull crack open on the road. He managed to slam his knee into the man's stomach, his wheeze of surprise coming just as Abby's voice broke through the roar in his ears.

An engine screamed furious and metallic in the distance.

"Dan! Dan, look out! *Go!*"

Dan glanced up from Finnoway's rumpled and dirtied shirt to see the single bright light of a motorcycle racing toward them. Black. The rest of it was black. That single light flew toward them in a blur of midnight steel.

Finnoway seized his chance to pin Dan to the ground. He reached behind him and pulled out a knife, his face its own terrible mask of many years of rage.

He moved to strike, but Dan rolled hard to the left, toward the curb with Abby and Jordan. He was still riding out the last of that momentum when he heard the quick *pop-pop* of tires colliding with bone and flesh, and the collective gasping shriek from everyone in the street.

He didn't want to turn and see what was left of Finnoway. It wouldn't be something he wanted to carry with him. The pain surged up in earnest now, his whole body spasming from the blows he had taken. Abby and Jordan were lifting him up out of the gutter and into a kneeling position, holding him aloft just long enough for him to smile faintly at the disappearing rider, a burst of engine smoke obscuring her escape.

"Dan? Can you hear me? Dan?" Abby shook him roughly, but his light was going out.

"Dan? Someone call an ambulance. Dan! Please, someone help us. . . ."

Chapter 44

A small, soft hand held his, squeezing him back to life. Dan blinked once, twice, letting the blue-white haze of the hospital room come into focus gradually. His head fell to the right, buoyed by a heavenly soft pillow, and there he found Abby, tucked against the hospital bed with her palm cradling his. His right palm. Some of the bandages had been removed and lessened, he saw with a thick gulp, and they showed more clearly the outline of his missing finger.

"Am I going to prison?" he wheezed.

That brought a relieved round of laughter from the trio gathered around his bed. Uncle Steve stood at the foot of the bed, out of his robe and slippers and looking healthy except for a few fading bruises. "Finnoway was waving a gun in the street like a lunatic while one of his pals pushed a teenager off a roof. That's not something you can cover up with a few bribes," Steve said, winking. "But I think you knew that, didn't you?"

"I had a good feeling," Dan whispered. "The motorcycle was a nice touch, though."

"Hit-and-run," Jordan said with a disbelieving shake of his head. "Not sure if there's such a thing as a *lucky* hit-and-run, but I'll take it."

"How did you know where to find me?" Dan asked. "I thought

you would all be at the police station."

"The *Metairie Daily*," Abby said, "if you can believe it. When I called them in a panic, they thought I was a crazy person. But not long after that, they got an anonymous tip from a 'trusted source' who said to call us, said you were being held under the old funeral home. We came as fast as we could."

Thanks, Mom.

"Police raided the building," Abby told him, stroking his hand gently. "I don't know if the Bone Artists are gone for good, but I'm sure the story will run in the papers soon. I bet Maisie's coworkers are eager to give her memory some peace," she said. "And Finnoway himself is dead."

"And Oliver?" Dan braced for the answer. He had no idea if a fall like that was even survivable.

"They're not sure if he'll walk again," Jordan said, leaning onto the bed just slightly behind Abby. "Again, not sure if you'd call that luck, but . . ."

"I think I'm glad he's alive." Dan nodded, realizing the weightlessness in his body was from the IV hooked into his arm. Whenever that stopped, he had a feeling his back would ache for weeks and weeks. "And I'm really not going to prison?"

Part of him couldn't believe it. He didn't *think* he was capable of murder, but Finnoway's setup had been so ironclad—and Dan's mind had been so scattered lately—there was a moment there when even he had believed he'd killed Tamsin.

"Some of his 'employees' were bending over backward to rat on him and avoid getting charged as accomplices to his crimes," Uncle Steve said, leaning onto the metal bedframe. "We'll see how long it takes for the police to figure out how deep Finnoway's influence goes, but it sounds like he's done this sort of thing before."

Dan shuddered, remembering the terrible chill of that dark interrogation room and the sound of teeth spilling across a metal table.

"I'm sorry I ruined our trip, and . . . I hope I didn't mess things up too badly for you here, Jordan," he murmured, trying to squeeze Abby's hand back. The drugs singing through his veins made his limbs feel detached, but he saw his fingers tighten around hers. His friends looked like they hadn't slept in days, dark circles smudged under their eyes.

Still, Jordan mustered a smile, resting his arms flat on the mattress and laying his head down on them. "You two still have a few days left. Once you're out of this bed we can probably sneak in a few hours of fun. And I still need help setting up my room. And there are like a thousand Xbox games you need to catch up on."

Dan shook his head slowly, looking from Jordan to Abby and then down at his bandaged hand. "No, I think I need to go home as soon as I can. I owe Paul and Sandy an explanation . . . for a lot of things." He paused, reveling in the weightless feeling keeping the pain at bay. For a second, things were kind of all right, and he wanted to remember how it felt. "Thanks for coming back for me," he added.

"I don't know what we would've done without the tip, Dan," Abby continued, entwining her fingers with his, "but we would've done *something*."

"I know," he whispered, leaning back against the pillows and feeling himself start to drift. "Thank you."

Epilogue

*T*he university was like a little slice of history and old-world charm. The campus and the neighborhood around it felt like they were from a bygone era, but thirty minutes on the El and the fast, dirty bustle of Chicago sprang up to pull you out of the academic bubble. It suited Dan just fine, the feeling that while the campus might be old, something new was always just a stone's throw away.

It wasn't anything like New Hampshire College, tucked away as it had been in that little hilltop city, isolated and lonely. Here he could watch the colors change, walk beneath old stone arches, and get just about the best pho a kid could hope for.

And that he was doing, maybe too much. But putting on a few pounds would go a long way to making Paul and Sandy worry less. He had toyed with the idea of joining a gym, thinking it might impress Abby if he showed up to visit her looking less like a string bean and more like a linebacker.

He had taken to bringing a blanket and his bag to the Midway Lawn to study. Being surrounded by the wide open greenery and the trees transitioning from green to gold reminded him of the better parts of being at NHC. Sometimes he wished Abby and Jordan were right there with him, walking to class like they had once done—Jordan teasing Dan about his hopelessly ugly clothes, and Abby trying to keep them from getting into a real fight.

At least he'd get to show Abby a bit of his life in Chicago soon. He was already the darling of his history class, which he didn't want to brag about, but which he knew Abby had picked up on during their Skype conversations. A family friend had invited Abby to join an artist's commune for a semester in Minnesota, which worked well with her decision to take a year and work on cataloging their adventures in a photo essay to show at a little gallery in the spring. She wanted him to visit her in New York for winter break, but getting Paul and Sandy to go along with that would be difficult, to say the least.

They knew everything now. For better or worse, they knew everything. It had made things a little easier, in the end, and after the tears and confusion and long talks into the night, Dan felt unburdened. They knew, and he didn't have to lie about his finger or who his birth parents had been or what he had seen at NHC. . . . It had been the last test of their love for him, and it still shocked and amazed him that they had passed it with flying colors.

Dan's phone buzzed on the plaid blanket. He grabbed it and huddled down into his scarf, a bitter wind coming off Lake Michigan.

Hey dork, u going 2 MSP for fall break? U should. Gonna see Abs & then I'm flying to NYC. Cal is dragging me 2 some dumb show. He is the worst. Come visit 2, miss u.

He grinned down at the text, feeling a pang of regret that he wouldn't get to go and watch Cal and Jordan in action. Apparently they were doing the long-distance thing (usually via a video game) and it was working out just fine.

Oliver and Sabrina stayed in touch, but only sparingly. All three of them were happy to discover that once Micah's remains were recovered from the funeral home and buried properly, the messages stopped. They still couldn't agree on whether it had been Micah's ghost or some kind of omniscient hacker, but in the end, Dan decided it didn't matter. They had brought his spirit peace.

Dan slept better. He dreamed better. Even though the occasional image from the past year bubbled up to haunt him, that's what therapy was for. Lots and lots and lots of therapy.

Now, Dan sent his regrets to Jordan, promising to visit soon, although he didn't quite know when that would be.

The wind rippled across the park again, frightening dog walkers back down the paths and toward home. Dan looked out in the direction of the water for a second and then began packing up, preferring to finish his studying inside where it was warm. He shoved his books back into his canvas bag and stood, folding up the blanket and wedging that into his pack, too. His phone tumbled out of his grasp, bouncing on the grass below.

"Here."

He nearly knocked heads with a woman, her red hair whipped around her face by the wind. She grabbed his phone with a woolly white glove and stood, gazing down into his face with the strangest expression. Dan felt a tremor pass from his nose all the way to his toes. He knew her face, and his hand froze as he opened his palm to take the phone.

"Hello, Daniel," she said softly, shyly. She pushed the fiery hair out of her face, sweeping it behind cold-reddened ears.

Her eyes were pale, pale blue, and she had a black motorcycle helmet tucked under one arm.

"Mom." He tried the word out. It sounded different when he said it to her, tentative but also relieved. "You're . . ."

Dan hugged the backpack to his chest, feeling small and terrified.

"You know why I had to stay away, right? You understand. . . ." Evelyn Ash trailed off, pressing her lips together tightly. "I'm not here to interfere with your life. You've done amazingly well on your own so far. No thanks to me."

"I wasn't on my own," he said defensively, but he couldn't keep up the chilly façade. He wanted to ask her so many things, just ask and ask until all of the questions he had stored up for eighteen years were finally out of him.

He wondered if maybe he owed her something of an apology for using her as a bargaining chip with Finnoway. But he had been right, hadn't he? She could handle herself, and she did, taking the Artificer out of the picture for good.

That was something to be thankful for, even if part of him wanted to snap at her, punish her somehow for abandoning him the way she had.

"No, of course not. And, well, if you want me to go away and never come back, I will." A tear escaped one of her eyes and she brushed at it impatiently. "God knows I've done it before. But I didn't want to, Daniel."

"I usually go by Dan," he murmured.

"Dan," his mother replied slowly, as if testing out the name. "Do you think I could walk with you? Just for a little while? I'll go if you ask me to."

"No!" he said, too quickly. Now that he had her there, well, the urge to scream at her was weaker than the urge to know her. Like her. She had made hard decisions, but hadn't he done the same? For his friends, for himself . . . "I mean, let's . . . let's walk. I'm this way." Dan gestured toward the walking path that circled back toward his dorm. "I knew it was you," he said after a while. "The anonymous tip? The motorcycle? I wasn't sure if you would still be around when I got to the street, but I knew it was you."

"I'm not surprised. You're obviously very clever. How did you know?"

They kept a meandering pace. Dan wasn't keen to get to his destination too quickly. This could very well be the first and last time they met, he thought; there was always a chance she could disappear again. "There was a picture of you and Dad in Finnoway's basement. You were wearing a motorcycle jacket. I recognized the symbol."

"I wished every day I could reach out to you," Evelyn whispered with a shivering sigh. "I couldn't risk it. But when I found out you were going to New Orleans, to *his* domain . . ."

"You were the one who pulled me out of Finnoway's clinic, too, weren't you? The good Samaritan," he said. "He didn't know it was you because you kept the helmet on."

"Like I said, clever." She grinned, then looked closely at his hand and the smile faded away.

"I bet it felt good to run over that jerk," Dan muttered.

"You have *no* idea."

"Yeah," he said with a dry laugh, glancing at his hand. "I kinda do."

Too soon they were back at his dormitory, standing under one of the yellowed arches carved with elaborate scalloped points. "So this is me." He dug his toe into the ground, searching for something profound to say. "Can we . . . can we maybe do this again? I don't know if you're staying in town or whatever but . . . I'd like to see you again. Get to know you. Get to know about Dad."

"Sure, yeah, Marcus would . . . God. You look so like him," she said gently, reaching out to touch his hair. Then Evelyn turned and ducked her head a little, tucking one stand of red hair behind her ear. She gave a wave and started back down the road. "Take care, Dan, sweetheart. I'll be seeing you real soon."

Acknowledgments

First, I have to thank the long-suffering Andrew Harwell, my editor, who is always willing to listen patiently while I work through insane plot ideas and blubbering what ifs. He makes my writing better, cleaner, and scarier, and for that I will be eternally grateful. I also want to acknowledge the major contribution of Kate McKean, who is as patient, understanding, and realistic as an agent can be. The team at Harper always outdoes itself with the beautiful design and photos, and they are hugely responsible for the atmosphere in these books.

To my family and friends, who listen to my griping, moaning, and fears, thank you for believing in me and lending your support. I am extremely fortunate to have such an amazing team behind me. Mom, Pops, Nick, Tristan, Julie, Gwen, and Dom, you can't be thanked often or intensely enough for the faith you've put in me and my writing. To Michelle, thanks for becoming such an amazing influence and mentor—you made some of the crappiest parts of this year bearable. To Steve, Kai, and Katie, thank you for pulling me out of the house and making sure I didn't starve or go too stir-crazy.

And finally, I have to thank the readers and fans who have turned *Asylum* into such a success. I'm constantly humbled by the outpouring of love and interest, and I have to pinch myself every day to have any of it make sense.

The images in this book are custom photo illustrations created by Faceout Studio and feature real found photographs from New Orleans.

⁓⁂⁓

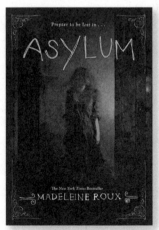